THE ROOMMATE

A dark and twisty psychological thriller
with an ending you won't forget

CAROLINE MACON
FLEISCHER

Joffe Books, London
www.joffebooks.com

First published in Great Britain in 2022

This book is a work of fiction. Names, characters, businesses, organizations, places and events are either the product of the author's imagination or are used fictitiously. Any resemblance to actual persons, living or dead, events or locales is entirely coincidental. The spelling used is American English except where fidelity to the author's rendering of accent or dialect supersedes this.

Cover art by Nick Castle

ISBN: 978-1-80405-434-5

For my roommates, Andy and Augie

CHAPTER ONE: CALIFORNIA

They arrived in Topanga on a cool October morning. Donna rode in the passenger seat and her mom Addie drove, the redwoods passing slower and slower until the creaky old U-Haul finally came to a stop. Donna clutched her Polaroid and stared eagerly out the window. There was her new house — a turquoise bungalow, of all things, tucked away in a neighborhood that seemed sparse but friendly enough.

Donna stuffed her hair into a ponytail and got out of the truck. Feeling stiff at the end of the long trip, she stretched her calves while she eyed the house. It was almost impossible to wrap her brain around the fact that this place was hers. It was a gift she never expected but had come just when she needed it most. At twenty-five, Donna had been busy wondering what the point of her life was — then, the promise for a better future came written in the deed to her elusive Grandmother Rudy's west coast home.

Addie squeezed Donna tight and let out a squeal. Compared to most Chicago houses, the place seemed enormous. It was built of turquoise-painted hardwood with tiny patches of moss peeking through the slats. A hand-laid stone path led the way from the street to the front porch, hedges of tall grass bordering the walkway. Two old flower boxes hung from the front windows. From them, a lazy and dry-looking assortment of petunias and ivy swung lightly in the wind.

In the front yard, there was a patchwork of three-by-three raised garden beds. The plots were overgrown — no one had tended to them in a while. Donna couldn't wait to get her hands in the dirt. Gardening was a hobby she always wanted to try but had never had a crack at. In each of the beds, there was greenery that signaled hope. A proud and confident tomato plant stood alone in one. It looked stubborn, ruthless. Donna loved it and took a photo of it with her Polaroid.

The front door of the house was painted a nice dusty blue. The doorknob was a glistening shade of turquoise — it looked crystal, almost. The porch was true hardwood, so dark it was almost black. Rudy had left a set of furniture on the front porch. One tiny table and one tiny chair and a little turquoise ashtray. The setup was perfect for a single woman.

On the ground lay an abandoned pair of Rudy's slippers. Donna's stomach turned when she saw them collecting moisture and dirt. She thought of a postcard Rudy sent her for Christmas one year, a photograph overlooking Topanga's twinkle-lit homes. Donna must have thrown it away at some point, unaware of its future significance. Postcards, slippers — these were the things of being human, things that people eventually leave behind when they die.

Addie lit a cigarette and plopped down in the chair. Letting her rest, Donna grabbed the slippers and went to investigate the back garden. As she got farther along the side of the house, the sun began to beat down harder. Sweat tingled on her scalp. The back gate was closed, but Donna looked in through panels of the fence. The backyard was almost barren, which she found a bit bizarre. She was curious, with the limited knowledge of gardening she did have, why the garden boxes were in front and not out back, where the light was much stronger.

She made it to the alley and tossed the slippers carelessly into the can. She wanted to make a moment of it but felt it was too sentimental. The house was her new start or whatever, and she didn't want to kill the mood with some kind of funeral. She tended to lean into dark feelings — in California, she was determined to home in on the positive.

But as she went back to join her mom, one more thing struck her as unusual. It was the casual aesthetic of the bungalow's side door. It looked strange, as though it didn't belong to the house. It was a cheap knockoff wood, unfinished, and purchased from somewhere like IKEA. The color was light and tacky. The windows were fingerprinted. The knob was drab. Donna wondered why her grandmother would take such care with the turquoise knob on the front door and not match it with the side knob.

"Hey, Mom?" she called. "Mom!" She didn't hear an answer. She circled to the front and found Addie up from her seat, moving a few boxes from the truck to the porch.

"Ready to see the inside?" Addie asked. "I didn't want to go in without you."

* * *

Donna turned the crystal turquoise doorknob and they entered the house. Something about the foyer instantly displeased her. She expected wafts of her grandmother's perfume, the feeling that everything was left in its proper place. Not only did everything seem slightly out of place, but the air smelled musty like a college apartment, or a man cave, or just a plain cave — Donna couldn't decide. In any case, the foyer reeked of phony hospitality. The umbrella stand by the door was fuzzy with dust. The pampering mirror above the key bowl was fingerprinted. There were specks of mud on the floor tiles.

"Isn't it beautiful?" Addie cooed. "Oh, Donna, it's perfect for you." She sighed loudly. "I'm jealous!"

It really was beautiful, Donna thought, but mostly in its essence. The framework was strong and the ceilings were high. The space was entirely open, except for the bedrooms.

The room was wide and neatly laid out — like the inside of a well-made snow globe. Knickknacks from her grandmother's travels decorated the counters.

All the objects fit a certain theme that seemed to reflect Rudy's individuality. Rudy was stoic and particular, which her home reflected, but it also gave Donna a glimpse at her more colorful side. A wicker basket sat full of handheld gardening tools. The mosaic pots Rudy had artistically curated now harbored dying plants, but Donna could imagine the calm the room evoked when everything was alive.

The walls were all different shades of turquoise. The cabinets were crisp and black. Donna spotted a matching teapot on the stove she couldn't wait to use. By the sofa, there was a well-rifled copy of an *ABA Journal*. In the trash can, there was trash. It didn't smell like it had been there too long, thankfully, even though she knew it had.

For some reason, the place — while boldly decorated — had a sense of gloominess, which suited Donna nicely. Above the wood fireplace sat a framed photo of Donna with her mother and father — a nuclear family that was so temporarily together. In the picture, they were at Chicago's Lincoln Park Zoo. It must have been taken in the mid-'90s — her father left them when Donna was only five. Looking at a rare photo of her young self gave her the chills. She wondered what animals she saw that day. What they ate for lunch. Suddenly wanting a sense of ownership over her new space, she felt eager for her mother to leave.

"I'm jealous," Addie repeated with a pout. "I guess we can start to bring in the stuff."

It only took a few trips. The house was furnished, after all, and Donna was starting life mostly from scratch. Before moving, she had taken a trip to the thrift store and found a knockoff Turkish rug, an old creaky box, and a gilded full-length mirror. The collection was Donna's haphazard attempt to add her own touches. On her grandmother's dresser top, she placed her Polaroid camera and Vaseline for her dry lips.

With everything in its place, she swiftly changed from her daytime comfy clothes into her nighttime comfy clothes and inspected herself in the full-length mirror. Since college, she felt like nothing fit right. She sighed and ran her fingers along a row of stress pimples along her lower jaw. Her nails were untidy, her socks didn't match, and her brassy blonde shag fell exhaustedly around her bare face.

Addie wanted to help her nest more, but Donna insisted she would settle in on her own later. The two opened a bottle of white and lay side by side in the great big master bed. Everyone in Chicago had begun referring to the house acquisition as Donna's "new leaf." When Donna heard the phrase "new leaf," she wanted to picture the green buds of spring. Instead, she always thought of the new leaves on the ground in fall — the crunchy brown ones that get trampled and snowed on and spat on.

Despite this self-doubt, Donna was elated to live somewhere new and think new thoughts and prove everybody wrong. She had been so cold and despondent in Chicago, accused of being aimless for many years. Her choice to pursue general studies at a local college — and take way longer than she should have to graduate — didn't help her case. Then, her job as a receptionist at a dentist's office had been migraine-inducing with its fluorescent lights and stressed-out clients.

But there in her brand-new home, Donna felt fresh and eager as a worm, ready to gobble up the compost in her life and make something new. Something that could, something that could — well, she didn't know. But she did know this west coast hideaway offered mysterious peace. She watched the redwoods move subtly in the breeze and eventually drifted off to sleep.

CHAPTER TWO: THE SNAKE

On the first night in her new bed, Donna had a nightmare about the IKEA door. There wasn't a lot to the dream, but it left her petrified. It was a pseudo-terror in which the side door had been left ajar. That was all. But the image alone left her rattled.

After some tossing, she got up to fetch a glass of water and check on the door. Addie was fast asleep on the couch, as the spare room didn't have a bed yet. Donna tiptoed past her. The door was securely shut and locked — just as she thought. Outside, nothing but a quiet, empty side yard. She went back to bed and pulled the quilt tightly around her in security. Thoughts racing, it took an hour to fall back asleep.

When she got up again, it was earlier than sunrise. She was so tired her head pounded. She stumbled into the kitchen and geared up the standard Mr. Coffee. Her mother was missing from the couch now, sitting on the porch with a cigarette and a far-off look.

"Do you want coffee?" Donna asked, joining her mom outside.

Addie jumped. "You scared the crap out of me! Why are you awake?" she said, pushing her brunette bangs back. Donna realized Addie had a small tear moving down her cheek.

"Why are you crying?" Donna asked. "Are you okay?"

"Sorry," Addie said and laughed, wiping the tear away. "I could barely sleep. I got so sad thinking of leaving you. You're going to be so far away."

"I know," Donna said. Next time she had a nightmare, her mom's presence wouldn't be there for comfort. She sat quietly on the arm of the patio chair and lit a cigarette for herself.

* * *

Later that morning, the two women returned the truck and picked up a rental car for Donna, a temporary solution until she bought her own. It was a little red Camry that Addie dubbed "the chili pepper car." Once they had the car, they drove to Burbank to part ways. Donna thanked Addie for all the help and cheerfully kissed her goodbye, but driving off in the chili pepper alone made her feel unsettled. After the side door incident, Donna was tempted to ask her mom to stay longer but suppressed it. She wanted to prove she could do it alone, plus the logistics would be a nightmare. While Addie's boss at the accounting firm was flexible, Addie was too proud to take much time off work. Their few-day road trip would have to suffice.

Donna was on edge. Since Rudy died, she felt like she was going through a dull replica of the bereavement process, but what she was grieving was her alienation from her father and her father's family. Donna had planned to go out and visit Rudy one day, but one day, as it so often does, never happened. Then, Rudy was gone, and Donna was left feeling guilty — why didn't she make more of an effort with her grandmother?

"To be fair," Addie had said as they dissected the will, "Rudy wasn't the warmest. If you had gone to see her, I'm sure she wouldn't have known what to do with you."

It was probably true. Donna's father had left the family when Donna was young. He had ghosted them before ghosted was even a term, and Addie's desperate, loud, late-night phone calls to him never did much to wear him down. Ultimately, Addie decided he was a narcissist, but Donna wasn't sure — she attributed her damaged childhood to the fact that love is complicated. That was the only reasoning able to get her through. And even though Donna's dad rarely called, he made all his child support payments to keep her alive and even thriving. While his departure caused her and Addie immense pain, it hadn't ruined them. In any case, he had been long estranged before he eventually died of cancer. The news came as a surprise to everyone in the family — his parents as well as Adelina and Donna. No one had heard much from him in his final days.

For that reason, Rudy leaving her home to Donna ten years later was even more perplexing. But at six feet tall and with a blade-sharp collarbone haircut, Rudy had a distinct, if not unforgiving, way of doing things. She probably rationalized that Donna was the only cousin in the family left unaccounted for. Donna was young, didn't yet have a family, and had wasted her potential on self-doubt. With more hands-on guidance from extended family, maybe her aspirations would have panned out more clearly. But in her family's relative alienation, Donna felt Grandma Rudy and that whole side of the family was a missed opportunity she hoped to rectify, starting with her move into the house. As a first step, Donna had a great aunt in SoCal, Sheeba, who lived only a short drive away. She planned to call her up once she got settled.

These were the thoughts that Donna circulated as she drove home through the California hills. To her frustration, the inaugural drive alone on Ventura Freeway wasn't dreamy. It was stressful. She was heavy-footed in the chili pepper car and almost crashed it into a gang of slowly moving cyclists. When she pulled over in Summit Valley to catch the views, none of it seemed right.

It was almost 10 a.m. and Donna had nothing to do but go home.

She made her way back to the bungalow in hopeless traffic. When she arrived, she pulled onto the parking pad in the back. "This is home now," she told herself. "Chill out. You're just going home."

Getting out of the car, she toyed with Rudy's house keys as she walked towards the house. It was a personal collection of souvenir keychains all tangled up with the lanyard. A miniature cross-stitch of a Valentine's heart. A small fabric hanky from New Mexico. A tiny, unlabeled jar of glittering sand. Donna was inspecting the keys so closely she almost didn't see it: outside the IKEA door lay a long, shedded snakeskin.

The skin was in three parts, approximately six feet long each. It was an unflattering shade of tan with splotches of brown and black. What worried Donna the most about the skin was how closely it matched the earth. It looked like skin that would be perfect for a creature who was trying to hide. She didn't know what was worse — three snakes that were six feet long or one snake that was almost twenty feet long. Thinking about all the variations gave her goosebumps.

She bent down to try to pick up the skin and gagged. As she got closer and saw each scale, her insides flipped. She thought of the snake this had once belonged to — the fangs, the tiny black bead eyes, the wide, wide head.

Its size made Donna think the animal was domestic. In a residential neighborhood, a wild snake of such size didn't seem realistic. Topanga was known as the "Snake Pit," but for rattlesnakes and seedy residents from the seventies — not twenty-foot-long pythons. But who knew — all the friendly feelings Donna had about California began to dissipate. Maybe it wasn't a cozy land of contemplative trails and Vitamin D. Maybe it was a dangerous safari. A human-versus-animal war zone.

Donna took a picture of the snake skins with her Polaroid. Then, she went to find kitchen tongs — they were all she could think of — to remove them. She delicately grabbed the skins with tongs and hopped on her tiptoes to the trash. She threw the skins and the tongs in the trash. She would never be able to eat a salad with those things again.

So later that evening, when she did have a salad for dinner, she awkwardly scooped the leaves out of the plastic container with a fork. Her grandmother had left all dishes behind, but Donna couldn't bear to use any of them. The home didn't feel like hers yet, especially with unusual animals crawling about. In a battle between Donna and a wild animal, she knew who would win — her humanity made her feel inferior, and her hair stood on end all night.

CHAPTER THREE: JOSHUA FLOWERS

Donna quickly became confused and depressed in California, slowing her "new leaf" process as well as the more practical process — like finding a job — down to almost nothing. The bills began to stack up immediately, and with no plans or anyone to hold her accountable, she felt like most of LA would think she was dressing like a homeless person.

In Chicago, big holey sweaters and boots were acceptable. In California, they were not. At grocery stores, she stood out like a goth in a crowd of preps. The crowd was pretty much two categories — peaceful retirees and content young families. The women her age that lived in Topanga already seemed so accomplished — musicians, artists and writers with supportive parents and coddling partners. The children in the neighborhood were clean, rosy-cheeked and put together. Donna was okay-looking when she tried, but she knew she needed a proper skin exfoliator and a pair of flattering trousers.

She wanted to look like an Instagram model but knew it was unrealistic. Still, knowing she needed to make a change, she took herself to TJ Maxx and settled on a few confidence-boosting outfits, an overpriced bottle of coconut sunscreen, and a tinted lip gloss. She was fresh-faced and thick. *Thick*. She hated the word, even if it was becoming popular. After years of being called thick in a bad way, her neck prickled now when people used it on her in a friendly way. It wasn't because she didn't appreciate thick bodies, but because she didn't appreciate her body at all. No masturbation — she barely even knew how to orgasm — no manifestation, no self-love. She was a repressed Midwesterner with a stifled curiosity for the finer things, like carefully curated pastel objects and nostalgic vintage photographs.

Desperate to get the electricity and gas in her name, Donna finally landed a job as a receptionist at a local, boutique hair salon. The conditions were strict. The owner, Lydia, was also from Chicago and was impressed by Donna's administrative intuition and "friendly voice — that will be great for fielding calls" but less-than-impressed with her sense of style. "Make a decided effort with your 'look' and you'll do great."

Being in a salon forced Donna to investigate her appearance every day, and it was a welcome opportunity to get out of the house. After the initial hire, Lydia only commented on her clothing decisions once ("pack heels if you can"), and the day-to-day routine helped Donna's psychology and balance. In her new reality, Donna quickly realized she'd taken everyday help for granted in Chicago — a quick trip to Macy's with her mom for winter boots shopping and Garrett Popcorn, or zipper assistance and spaghetti-strap-tightening from a friend. In this new environment, small fashion mishaps had no resolution. Snagged zippers remained stuck, Donna fumbling and tripping around awkwardly until she gave up. However, while the fashion stuff seemed arbitrary, cash was tight so that every polished detail added up. She needed to make some more money to survive in the way she wanted to survive. And every obstacle in the way to doing so made her feel more uncomfortably alone.

So one night, cozied up in her grandmother's bed — she still thought of it as her grandmother's bed — Donna decided to search for a roommate. She heard strange things about finding a roommate on Craigslist, but she also heard positive things. The moochy troll she lived with during her undergrad years had been from a Facebook group, so Craigslist seemed as promising as anything else.

She dialed up her mom to explain what she was going through. "I'm going to find someone on Craigslist," she said, "just for a while."

Addie sighed heavily. "Donna, why?"

"I need help with bills," Donna insisted.

"I can send you some money if you need it—" Addie went on, "but only for the short term."

"It's more than that," Donna admitted. "I just feel lonely."

"Of course you are, Donna." Her mom sounded impatient. Donna tried to shake the feeling that she was a disappointment and took a deep inhale. Then exhale, two, three, four. "But you need to be careful," Addie went on. "Vet them thoroughly." It was a strict command. And, as her mom went on, Donna zoned out on the side door.

Sometimes, in the empty house, she could swear she heard someone else tiptoeing around inside, listening to her every move. Sometimes she swore she placed something in one place and then found it somewhere else. After her first big grocery trip, Donna was surprised by how quickly she went through the package of toilet paper on her own. She purchased a twelve-pack and expected it to last longer. She attributed her strange feeling to anxiety over exceeding her budget in those early days alone — but still, sometimes there were unfamiliar smells in the house, feelings, shifts. Even then, on the phone with her mother, she felt like she was being watched. She tried to shake it off as paranoia but felt, strangely, like someone was with her.

"You're on your own." Her mom was still talking. "And that's the beauty of it. I'd give anything to have a fresh start like that."

"It's just temporary," Donna said. "I just need someone temporarily." Then, her mom hung up. It was aggravating, but Donna knew what she needed and knew her mom would come around if she found the right person.

She thought of a few details about herself that may be pertinent to know.

"I am a friendly young professional," she wrote.

Dear Everyone,

I am a friendly young professional. I am not much of a partier but do enjoy long conversations over cheese plates and things like that. I am fun. I do like a good drink.

I work during the day and am usually home at night. I am open to having a roommate with a different schedule, so long as they are respectful of my rest time. I am not opposed to guests, but I also don't love having them. If there are guests, I just like notice.

I won't brag about how neat and tidy I am because I am not. I am also not a pig. If you are a pig, it will not be a match. If you are uptight, it will also not be a match.

Bonus points if you can garden — I am trying to redo some things around here to make it more my own.

You will have a guest bedroom in a quaint, stylish, turquoise-themed cottage. We will be sharing a bathroom, so I prefer a female though I am open to any gender.

Mostly, I just want someone to be around that doesn't feel bad to be around. I had some bad experiences in my previous city. I'm a dropout dentist receptionist and I want to begin a journey with someone new. We don't have to be best friends, but some kind of bond would be nice.

Yrs,
Donna – F – 25

She didn't post the address, but she posted a well-known intersection nearby. Then, she went to microwave a frozen Indian dinner. Butter chicken, her favorite. It had a low calorie count but tasted as if it had a high calorie count, creamy and with lots of rice. Admittedly, she also preferred microwave meals still so she didn't have to use any of Rudy's nice dishes. But also, Donna cared about her weight more since working at the salon. Most of the Californians who visited it to get their hair done were small and fit.

Donna's skin was olive and her hair was bleached. She had a nose ring she did not yet realize was not great for her face. Her hair's ends were still broken from years of using a blow dryer. It was wavy, but not in the beach-waves kind of way. As she waited for her butter chicken, she stood like a flamingo, like she always did, with one foot tucked into the crevice of her other leg's knee.

She was wearing jean shorts that were slightly too big, a burnt orange baseball tee, and a giant black cardigan that was also too big. On her flamingo feet sat two ankle-length socks that were the wrong color. Her butt was big and she was self-conscious about it, so she wore oversized clothing. As she waited for the chicken to finish in the microwave, she looked at her shape in the black reflective glass. Once, she took a quiz called "What Body Type Are You?" and the result was "Spoon." That was worse than a pear, she thought.

Soon, she would have a roommate and she could afford better food. When the machine beeped, she felt relief, opened the door and tore off the plastic. As she stirred the chicken, there was the ping of an email in the next room. Let the fun begin.

It was some girl named Claudia, and Donna barely read the message. Claudia's evidence for being a perfect roommate candidate included a batch of revealing selfies. Getting the vibe that this was not, in fact, a perfect candidate, Donna sent her to the waste basket.

She sat quietly and stared at the living room, imagining it to be full of people. It wasn't true she didn't like guests. In fact, Donna loved guests. She grew up in a home where her mom was constantly entertaining. No, it was something deeper than that. It was social anxiety, maybe, or the need to feel like she moved to a new place and thus needed to be professional. She saw a version of herself that lived in

California, and it was not the version of herself that lived in Chicago. Her Chicago self brought her a deep sadness, like someone who just couldn't figure it out. Someone who could have been happy, but just wasn't. Someone who could—

Her email pinged again.

It was from a man.

The man's name was Joshua Flowers.

The subject line of Joshua Flowers' email read, "Perfect Timing." The message was polite and eloquent.

Dear Donna,

I will warn you I do identify as a man so I may not be exactly what you are looking for. And admittedly, I am a little bit clean and uptight.

We do have some things in common, though. I like cheese plates, for starters. I also have mixed feelings about guests. Maybe if I move in we can say, no guests! Then revisit the subject after we both get some counseling?

I'm kidding.

In seriousness, your listing felt a little serendipitous. I've lived in the area for a long time and am not eager to leave. The thing is, however, someone just moved into my apartment who I don't . . . favor, to put it lightly. I miss having the place to myself! I am not against having a roommate, of course, but would prefer to get along properly.

Is there a time we could meet? It doesn't have to be at the house. We could grab a glass of wine or maybe some cheese? Or both? Let me know what you think, and we can discuss details.

Sincerely,
Joshua Flowers

P.S. I do really like turquoise, just FYI.

Joshua Flowers' email made Donna laugh. She hadn't laughed since her mother left town almost a month before.

The days were blurring together, and while Donna expected to feel more acclimated, she somehow felt like more of a mess. Everything was disorienting, from the grocery store to nights in front of the television. She was grateful for the opportunity to live here but worried about how she would feel one, two, or five years down the line. She wanted to meet Joshua, maybe he could be a friend.

Having a good feeling, she gave him a call. He answered right away with a gruff but warm-sounding voice. "This is Joshua," he said.

"Hi," she said. "It's Donna." She paused nervously. "From Craigslist."

"So, what do you think?" he asked.

"I think you sound — normal enough." She laughed. "Couldn't hurt to have dinner or something."

"Are you familiar with the area?" he asked. "What restaurants do you like?"

"I haven't been out to eat even once," she admitted. "Any recommendations?"

"That's a high bar," he said. "Now I want to impress you." He paused. "Hmm. Let's go to—" she heard Joshua tapping his hands in thought. "Let's go to Canyon Bistro & Wine Bar. It's like — well, it's about ten minutes from the intersection you listed."

"You free Sunday?" she asked. That was a few days away. She didn't want her schedule to sound too desperately open.

"Sure," Joshua said. "Let's do seven. I'll see you then."

So, they had a date for wine and cheese. If all went well at the bistro, Donna would agree to give Joshua a tour. Everything felt cordial and very grown up. Donna looked forward to it.

That night, Donna took a long shower and assessed what type of person she wanted to be. She was tired of moping. It was time to make moves. She decided to treat herself to a cut and color at the salon. Maybe once it happened, Lydia would pal up with her a little more. She also decided to get out more. She would get a bike. She would see the hills and the water and the sky. She would see more than turquoise and the insides of her eyes. She would see herself. She promised.

* * *

In the week before Joshua, Donna moved everything out of her grandmother's house and moved it back in. She hired a little help for the heavy things. She didn't want to disrespect her grandmother by buying new things, but she wanted the home to have her mark on it. It was the subtle changes that gave Donna vitality. The couches were in new places, and the side tables altered slightly. There were some new wall decorations, fresh houseplants to give the air life. She barely spent any money, but the place felt reclaimed.

She also made the kitchen more user-friendly, which to Donna meant less sophisticated. She wanted more space to cook her microwave dinners, less clutter and frills. She did purchase a new pair of tongs. She cleaned up the living room, keeping the *ABA Journal* on display. It was one of the last touches of her grandmother's besides the gorgeous wall paint color. On the front porch, she added a second chair she found in a nearby alleyway. It was as if God placed it there. It looked just like the other one.

The last thing she needed to tackle was cleaning up the guest bedroom. If it were going to be Joshua's, or whomever's, it needed a good spruce. When she entered the guest room, she noticed a strange smell. It didn't put her off, but it did leave an impression. It reminded her of the smell she felt the first day she walked in with her mother. It wasn't bad, just sort of dank. Dirtier than the rest of the house. She cleaned the room dutifully and patched the walls. She wanted it to have a fresh slate without art or hook hangers or anything.

It was still a home for a single woman, but perhaps a single woman with a companion. Donna missed the noise of her mother's house — people were always over for drinks and card games. Then in college, friends and frenemies constantly bustling in and out. Even if Donna hadn't found the deep connections she craved, she felt the most herself amidst the chaos of other people. She didn't do well alone, it turned out. She didn't do well alone at all.

* * *

When Donna arrived at the bistro, Joshua was waiting for her. He sat at a small table on the patio, so she noticed him right as she walked up. He didn't look how she expected — he was quite a bit older than she imagined. He was a small man with glasses and a bald spot. He wore a yellow and brown gingham button-down. There was a pen in his front pocket. His jeans were faded and a little tattered, and he wore brown shoes to match.

When she saw the wear on his shoes, she felt a sense of home. They reminded her of shoes in the Midwest, after a spring of clunking around in the light rain. He wore the biggest smile. It spread across his whole face and showed crooked, charming teeth like a happy Jack-O-Lantern. Donna felt relieved he was a little dressed up. She was too, but nothing crazy. She wanted to make a quality first impression on her potential roommate and friend.

"I ordered us a charcuterie," Joshua said. "I hope that's okay."

"Heck yeah," Donna said, taking off her bag.

"I figured we were on the same page about that," Joshua said.

"I basically responded to you just because of the cheese plate," Donna said and laughed.

They paused and looked at each other and smiled. Donna pulled a little at her cardigan.

"Thank you for meeting me," Joshua finally said. The waiter reached over him and set down the plate.

They debated splitting a bottle of wine, but Donna liked Chardonnay and Joshua liked Cabernet. After an awkward settlement, they settled on a bottle of rosé.

"I never order rosé," Joshua said.

"Me either," Donna agreed, and they cheered to that.

Then, they got to business. They talked about how much Joshua would pay. There was a little pushback, but the cost was average for the area, so Donna made him agree to see it first. She promised him it would be worth it. It was a great place, a quiet location, plus he wouldn't have to deal with the rigmarole of a landlord.

They talked about their quirks and things past roommates did that drove them crazy. "I have more experience than you," Joshua said, and Donna assured him he wasn't *that* old.

"How long have you lived here?" Donna asked after a peaceful pause.

"Oh, a while."

"How long is a while?"

"Hm." He hesitated. "A few months."

"That isn't a while!" she coughed.

"It is for me."

There was something mysterious like that about him, a calming quiet that left room for a lot of questions. He had a lot of questions for her, too. They had some surprising similarities in their lives. For example, they both were star volleyball players that were out of practice. Both enjoyed the beach and lying out in the sun. Both had somewhat of a dreary outlook on life and morbid senses of humor. Multiple jokes were made about the mustard on the charcuterie plate. It *was* bad mustard. Both praised the duck pate. It was the best part. Both nodded in enthusiasm when the waiter asked if they wanted more crackers.

"Do we have to pay for it?" Donna asked. The waiter said he would make an exception and winked. It was silly — they knew the crackers were free.

After a long while, the sun started to set and crickets began to chirp. It felt nice to Donna to spend time with someone again. Just quality, intentional time. The meeting was going well. Nearby, a woman was eating alone with her dog at her feet. The dog was small and old and didn't need a leash. Donna admired its loyalty and wondered if the dog had been so loyal as an active pup. She felt a little light from the alcohol. Not drunk, but just in a happy, clouded buzz.

"When did you get your haircut?" Joshua suddenly asked.

"How did you know I just got it cut?"

He laughed. "I mean it looks fresh."

"Thank you." Donna raised her glass. "It is."

Into the second half of the bottle of wine, the conversation became more serious. When the waiter cleared the plates, Joshua leaned onto the table with his two elbows and asked Donna, "What is one thing you absolutely don't want in a roommate?"

Donna thought hard. For the last week, she thought only of what she did want in a roommate and thought nothing of what she didn't want. "I like a space that has character," she said. "In that way, the house is ideal for me. Growing up, my house was kinda bland. My mom had to work a lot, or we were hanging out, so it was never all that decorated or anything. And without my dad, friendships became super important. Most of our friends in Chicago are like family — not knowing anyone in Topanga feels kinda weird. So, I guess one thing I don't want is coldness. Not like I want to live in a party house or anything, but I want someone to kick it with. No bad vibes—" she paused as realized she was beginning to ramble "— is the simple answer."

Joshua nodded in agreement. "Do you have any big fears?"

Donna liked Joshua. His questions stimulated her. And the fact that he kept asking them made her feel like she wasn't rambling at all.

"Snakes," she answered. Joshua raised his eyebrows. "It's a bit of a new thing, actually," she said. "Something happened that was kinda fucked up."

He nodded and took a sip of wine. "Go on."

Donna laughed and smoothed out her napkin on the table. "So, about a month ago, when I first moved in, I found a snakeskin out by the backyard."

"Like from a garden snake?"

"No," she snorted. "Like a fucking huge like twenty-foot-long snake."

"What?"

"Yeah, it was crazy. Like, I literally almost straight up packed my bags and left."

"So what, did you call animal control?"

"No — I didn't know what to do. I scooped it up with kitchen tongs and threw it in the dumpster."

Joshua laughed. "Are the kitchen tongs back in the drawer?" he asked. "Like, would we be eating salads with them?"

"I threw those away, too," Donna said. "Okay, I'm probably scaring you off. But in my defense, I didn't get the impression it was like, a common occurrence, okay?"

"Don't worry about it," Joshua said. "I'll buy you a new set of tongs."

"What about you?" Donna asked. "What's something in a roommate you just couldn't get over?"

Joshua drank his wine and played with his napkin a little, then the waiter came to drop off the check and he grabbed it. "I got this," he said. He paused for a second. "I just don't want anyone who's gonna stab me in the back."

* * *

They drove in separate cars to the house, Donna leading the way in the chili pepper. As she drove, she thought about how well it was going. She and Joshua had an immediate connection, like cousins, like family gone adrift. Even as he followed behind her in the car, something was natural. She debated stopping at the liquor store for more wine — she didn't have any at the house — but thought it was too strong a gesture. It had been so long since she talked to someone, really talked to someone, and she loved the ease of their interaction.

When they pulled up to the house, he was a step ahead of her.

"Maybe this is too strong a gesture," he said, just like he'd read her mind. "But I have this bottle of wine in my trunk I've been saving. A coworker gave it to me. Do you want to, like, hang out?"

Donna laughed and admitted she was on the same page. Her insecurities about coming off too clingy soon dissipated.

So, they went inside. Joshua looked a little surprised when he entered. Donna couldn't put her finger on why.

"It looks great in here," he said.

"What? You're surprised it's neat?"

"No . . ." He trailed off. "I expected it to be, um, a little more grandma-ish."

"I redid some things," Donna replied, "but really only used what I had."

"I like it," he said. "I like it a lot."

She showed him the house and where his room would be. He remarked on the high ceilings and the big closet. Moving into the kitchen, Joshua loved the sturdy cabinets and worn-in feeling. He was equally intrigued by the antique teapot on the stove. "That's fun," he said, "like an old relic." He put his hands on his belly and smoothed down his shirt a bit as he looked around. "You weren't lying," he said and sighed. "I think the place would be perfect."

They sat on the couch and opened the wine, and the conversation became more casual. Donna told Joshua all about her one and only boyfriend, Otto, how in retrospect there hadn't been much special about him — he was a simpleton, much too earnest, but Donna had been so sold on the idea that she was supposed to be dating that she repressed her disdain. Then, soon after the relationship's demise, she admitted to herself that Otto's unwavering niceness and constant cooperation was a bore, a death sentence. She craved the crackle and pop of a good disagreement, the sweaty, apologetic, cat-and-mouse sex afterward. Otto took the blame for everything — never accused Donna of any wrongdoing — and while many women would want to hug him for it, Donna wanted to smack him.

"We broke up at the end of college," she said. "My one and only love." She laughed darkly. "He moved on and went straight to grad school in another state. Got betrothed to a skinny nurse or something."

"I take it you weren't so sad," Joshua said.

"He was cute," Donna said. She hesitated to open up to Joshua about her desire for more drama but felt so comfortable in his presence. She leaned in close and wrinkled her nose. "Is it bad I always wanted like — you know, a boyfriend who made me break glass in the kitchen and raise my voice or something?" Her eyes glistened. "I always wanted to be in the street screaming like, 'I love you, baby!'"

"And it wasn't like that," Joshua said, smiling.

"No, no, it was not."

"I don't think it's a bad thing to want," Joshua said. "I, on the other hand, have had only those kinds of lovers with the yelling. I think some calm would do me good."

"Maybe we can help neutralize each other," Donna said, topping off his glass of wine.

"I haven't had a boyfriend in years," he said. "It's the bald spot. Chases them right away."

"No," Donna sympathized. "I think it's sweet."

"You should tell that to the guys," Joshua said.

Donna laughed. "I will."

When the conversation reached a natural lull, they went around the whole house again — Donna showed him this and that and told small stories about her grandmother's eccentricities. How she barely knew her at all, but one thing she did know was that Grandma Rudy made the best eggs and grits Donna had ever eaten. During Rudy's visits to Chicago, though there were only a few, she always made it a point to serve them for breakfast. Perfectly over-easy, creamy and buttery, with fresh chives on top.

"I can't believe you just got this house," Joshua said. "When you were so removed from her."

"It kind of came to me by default. I'm young, I'm single, and I was willing to move. I thought it would be fun."

"I wish something like that would happen to me," Joshua said, and there was an awkward silence. "I guess that's my only hesitation," he confessed, "about signing a lease with you. I'm afraid it's going to bother me, even though I know it's silly, to know that I am paying rent and you aren't. For the same space."

Donna felt a pang of negative energy. It went straight to her stomach. "That's how renting works," she said.

"I know," Joshua said, walking away slowly. "But if we become friends, it might be hard." He trailed off. "I know it's stupid. I just get nervous."

"Don't be nervous," Donna said. "I will make it as smooth as possible."

"You have any experience with stuff like this?" Joshua asked.

"Not one bit," Donna admitted, and they laughed. "What do you think?"

There was a long pause. The room felt a bit uncomfortable. Why would he seek out the apartment if he dreaded paying the rent? Was he really expecting to become so close that he would think about things like that? When Donna decided to get a roommate, she hadn't expected the negotiations to be so heavy.

"Let me think on it," he decided. "Can I let you know tomorrow?"

"Sounds like a plan."

"Okay," Joshua said. "I'm sorry for my honesty. It's weird though, just feeling like I can be honest with you."

They looked at each other for a long, long time.

"Here," Donna said. "Let me walk you out."

CHAPTER FOUR: TURQUOISE

The next day at the salon was a quiet Monday with very few appointments. On the slow days, Donna and Lydia had begun to develop a good talkative relationship. It was like back-and-forth therapy. That day, Donna was doing very little reception-ing and a lot of talking-about-Joshua-ing. Lydia thought he sounded off.

"Can't you find someone else?" Lydia asked. Lydia was about four foot eleven but wore shoes that made her six foot five. Today, she wore her hair natural in a leopard print clip at the top of her head. "I might know someone."

"Like who?" Donna asked.

"Like . . . anyone else," Lydia said.

"You looking for a place?" Donna asked.

"Fuck no," Lydia said. "I require living by myself. Thank you."

Donna was quiet and pretended to work for a second. Then she said, "I got a lot of emails, but this dude just stood out. I feel like we're cut from the same cloth or something."

"Maybe you are, but he said he would be jealous of you not paying for rent and that's scary."

"I get what he means, though," Donna rationalized. "Like in my previous apartment, I was paying more than my boyfriend, whose place was way nicer, and that really bummed me out."

"Donna. Your last place was a dump and your boyfriend was dudsville. Who cares?"

"Okay," Donna said, feeling defensive.

"On the other hand," Lydia thought about it for a moment, "I'm glad he was honest."

"Me too," Donna said. "That's kind of part of the appeal."

"At least you know he wouldn't be the type to, like, lay low and harbor resentment."

"Yeah," Donna said. She glanced around the deserted salon. "It's slow today."

"We got anyone else on the books?" Lydia asked.

"No . . ."

"Okay." Lydia turned to look at her. "I like your haircut. But I think if you want to really start new, you have to go bolder."

"Bolder how?" Donna asked, following Lydia to a chair.

Her new cut was cute. Less shaggy and more precise — the moppy layers of before had been transformed into a flattering face frame. It was the first time Donna had ever liked her jawline.

"Let's try a little color," said Lydia. "Have you been blonde your whole life?"

Donna had. When her natural blonde had begun to grow out in her teenage years, Donna had started a do-it-yourself at-home bleach regimen that would make any hairdresser cringe. When she left the salon that day, she had two turquoise streaks in her hair running down behind her ears.

* * *

Joshua emailed around eight that night. He said he was in. When Donna read the email, a wave of tension left her. Her financial strain of moving to California, her loneliness, and her fear of making a mess of her new life would find relief, at least for a while. She did worry about his threat of jealousy but assumed he had come around to the idea of renting. It was a weird thing to say, but she had said weird things before. She didn't want to be too judgmental.

Despite her calming feeling, as she fell asleep, she felt more alone than ever. She gave her mother a call, but Addie was out with friends. She considered texting Lydia, but it was too late at night. The shadows on the walls looked stark, the leaves like skeletons reaching down on her. Then she remembered the creepy side door. She couldn't stop picturing it. It was frozen in her head like an icon, attached to nothing. She got up to check if it was locked. It was. Strangely, she didn't have a key for it, so it could only lock from the inside.

She took a shot of bourbon to ease her anxiety and help her fall asleep, but her dreams were bizarre again. She was floating, floating, floating, and wanted to be solid. She needed to land on the Earth again soon.

In the morning, she awoke to a check from Joshua on the front porch. It was sealed in an envelope that was marked with a cat sticker and was tucked into the mailbox. There was no postmark — he'd taken the time to come by and deliver it himself. Her heart leapt. Not only had he agreed to room, but he'd paid the rent up front. There was no contract. There was no bullshit. They were beyond that. All the warnings she had heard about renting to a stranger were false. Here this guy was, completely reliable and willing to overcome his anxieties to make it work. She noticed his check had no address. It made sense — he moved around a lot, she figured, but something about the blank upper left corner seemed a bit eerie. She emailed him and said:

Thanks for the check! Are you sure you want me to cash it with no return address? I wanted to make sure but don't want to overstep your privacy.

Joshua responded promptly:

It's okay. We won't have much privacy for long, roomie. Why don't I go ahead and write you another? I'll put my new address as the return. :)

He said he could move in the next day. Donna would be at the salon. She offered to take off so she could help, but he assured her he didn't have a lot of stuff. "Don't go to the trouble," he said, "I'll find someone."

So, as requested, Donna didn't go to much trouble but did want to welcome him warmly. She gave him the lockbox code and hid keys for him in a small box on the fence. In the kitchen, she placed a bouquet of mixed flowers, a bottle of cheap champagne and a note that read, "Welcome home!"

* * *

Donna went straight home after her shift. When she arrived, the place was just as she left it — the champagne and flowers were still on the counter, but the keys were gone.

"I told you not to trouble yourself," Joshua said behind her, and she jumped. "Did I scare you?"

She laughed. "It was so quiet! I'll get used to having company."

"I'm not company, though," he said, and laughed.

"Do you like the flowers?"

"I love them."

"Here, I'll get you a vase," she said, opening the cabinet.

"Thank you. But please, leave them out here. We should both enjoy them," Joshua said.

"You sure?"

"Yeah. I don't like keeping much in my room anyway."

Donna looked around the space. She didn't see boxes or anything. "Where is all your stuff?"

"It's already in its place," he said.

"Seriously? Well, I cleared out some space for you in the bathroom."

"No need," he said. "I just have a toothbrush and deodorant. I figure we can just share toiletries. I'll buy next time."

"Okay," Donna considered. "It would be easiest."

"I got groceries for us, too," Joshua said, opening the fridge. "Help yourself to anything you like."

Donna opened the fridge and gasped. It was fuller than any time since she had moved in. The food looked delicious.

It was organized like her mother's always was — he was clearly someone who thinks of everything. She went to fix herself a snack. Strawberries and crackers with feta cheese and honey. All things she would rarely have considered purchasing, especially not all together.

"I'm being a pig," she said. "Want some?"

"No thanks," said Joshua. "I'm just getting settled."

He went into his room — no longer the guest room — and locked the door. He was so quiet, it was like he wasn't there. Still, it was nice to have a little background noise in the house. It made Donna feel safer.

As the night went on, Donna began to wish they could talk or something. She wanted to share the champagne and watch a movie. She was sure he was busy, unloading things, and didn't want to bother him. After much deliberation, she knocked on the door lightly.

"Joshua?" she asked quietly. "I don't want to bother you, but do you, um, want to watch a movie or something?"

He responded like he'd been waiting for her to ask the whole time. "That sounds great," he said. "Give me a minute and I'll come out."

When he joined her on the couch, the pair drank the champagne and sat with a comfortable distance between them. They binge-watched *Barefoot Contessa* and laughed at Ina Garten's unironic ability to make tying and roasting a whole lamb look simple. Donna had always loved Ina because she was everything Donna wasn't — self-assured, charismatic, precise. She was iconic, and Joshua agreed. After the champagne was gone and it had gotten later, they felt strange using the bathroom, one after the other. Donna felt she hadn't shared a bathroom in ages, even though it had only been a few weeks. They did not brush their teeth side by side. Joshua brushed his in the kitchen. When they said goodnight, they did a forced side hug.

"I'm glad you're home," Donna said, feeling cheesy.

"Me too, Mom," Joshua joked, and turned off the light.

Donna closed her door and went to sleep. It was the first night she slept well in this home. The shadows and sounds of the outside were welcome for once. She felt like she was in her right place. It was her room, not Grandma Rudy's. It was Joshua's room, not the guest room. His check cashed and the fridge was full of groceries. He was older, more mature. He preferred to date men, so she didn't need to worry about a romance. Everything felt like destiny.

Early in the morning, she woke to the sound of Joshua puttering around lightly. She heard him use the restroom, fix himself something to eat and go out for a walk. She dozed in and out of sleep, comfy under the quilt. About an hour after, Donna heard Joshua return.

But he came in through the side IKEA door, the one she didn't have a key for.

CHAPTER FIVE: THE SIDE DOOR

She pressed her ear to the wall to make sure she wasn't mistaken. But she heard him, clear as day, entering on the side of the house instead of the front. Maybe she had forgotten to lock it the night before. No, she remembered locking it vividly. There was no way.

She got fully dressed and prepared to go ask him. She smoothed down her hair, not wanting to seem like she slept in too much. She also corrected her face. She didn't want to look confrontational or creepy.

When she entered the living room, Joshua was on the sofa reading the *ABA Journal* and sipping coffee.

"Good morning," he offered, and Donna was quiet. "Do you drink coffee?"

"I do," she said. He began to get up. "Don't get up," she said. "I got it."

He cozied up again. He looked so comfortable. Donna eyed the side door. It was locked now. Had she imagined it? Maybe she wasn't hearing correctly.

"Can I ask you something?" she said. "Why did you come in through the side door this morning?"

"What do you mean?" he asked.

"I'm just asking because I don't have a key to it, and so I wondered how you got in."

"Oh," Joshua said. "It was unlocked."

Donna paused.

"Am I not supposed to use it?"

"No, you can use it, I just, I could have sworn I locked it."

"Well, you didn't, but if you prefer that I not use it, that's okay. We can keep it locked all the time."

"That's silly," Donna said. "We can leave it unlocked when we're home or we'll, I don't know, get a locksmith one day and get a proper key for it."

"Have I upset you?" Joshua asked.

"No. God no, not at all. I'm just a little weird about locked doors," Donna said. After a childhood with a single, working mom, it was true. "I never forget."

"We did stay up a bit late last night, and we did drink some champagne." Joshua paused. "Are you okay? I'm sure it's fine, Donna. Topanga is safe."

"No, I know," she said. "Sorry." She was embarrassed. She didn't mean to take him off guard.

"Why don't we call a locksmith?" Joshua asked. "It's on me."

"Please," Donna said. "You're my tenant. I should call the locksmith. Don't worry about it."

"Oh, I'm your tenant?" Joshua said and smiled. "I thought we were friends!"

"Shut up," Donna said playfully. She looked up locksmiths in the area. She had never called a locksmith before. She was horrified when she saw the cost. Welcome to SoCal.

* * *

The days went on peacefully for a while. The pair separated during the day, when Donna went to the salon and Joshua went to work as a "backend coder," as he called it. For a couple months, things did get easier for Donna, financially. Joshua paid his rent and bills on time. When issues around the house came up, she was able to afford the repairs. They now had a working key for the side door, but only Joshua used it. They both enjoyed watching the Food Network and would convene every other night or so to watch it together. Their relationship didn't deepen, per se, but gradually became more natural.

With the extra cash, Donna bought a used but well-working road bike. Donna had become attached to her Polaroid, even though the film was expensive, and she took shots of almost everything she passed on her bike. The cacti, the funny-looking boulders, the wonderfully depressing sunsets. Her camera and her bike had become her accomplices almost, joining her on every drunken exploration, every escapade. At times, she felt richly lonely and understood why her grandmother was so elusive. Her chilly Chicago heart was blossoming, and even as she lived in it, she was afraid she would never feel so deeply alive again. She finally traded in her chili pepper rental for a car that suited her better — a gently-used white Jetta that made her feel more professional. And on top of all the positive changes, Joshua was a nice accessory in Donna's life. His presence offered a stable, homey feeling.

"I'm glad things are going so well with Joshua," Addie said when they spoke on the phone. "But I do hope this is temporary. There is nothing like living by yourself."

Donna rolled her eyes. Even if it wasn't true, sometimes she felt like her mother did not get her at all.

One night, Donna was closing at the salon. She didn't usually close, but her fellow receptionist was an actress and had an irrefusable audition or something to attend. Closing included a few after-hours activities, such as doing the laundry and restocking the hair products. Feeling a bit tired and out of sorts, Donna put on some music and went to task.

As she was trying to reach a high shelf, she fell off the step stool and rolled her ankle. The pain was so excruciating, she could barely stand. Finally, she was able to get off the ground but couldn't put any weight on her left foot. She wept from the pain. First, she called Lydia, but it went straight to voicemail. She didn't know how she would get herself to the hospital and knew an ambulance would be expensive. She almost typed 911 but chickened out. Surely she could get herself to the hospital without it. She considered driving herself there — but even the thought of it traumatized her. There was no way she could drive; even getting to her parking space might injure her further.

It was late. She was certain Joshua would be home. She was embarrassed to call but knew he would come. He answered immediately and promised he would leave straight away.

Within minutes, he was knocking at the salon door. Donna was in tears on the floor, alongside the mess of hair supply boxes and spilled hair dye that had toppled when she fell. The dye had most definitely stained the floor, and she would have to pay for any supplies that were damaged. Her ankle felt like it was shattered, and she could only crawl to the doorknob to flick it open.

"Oh, honey," Joshua said. "Here, let me help you."

He picked her up and began to carry her to the car. "I'm going to get fired," she sobbed. "And I'm gonna have to pay for all this shit."

"Think about that later. We gotta get you to the hospital," Joshua insisted.

"Joshua, please," Donna begged. "Please switch the laundry on first and help pick up the boxes." Joshua did that as Donna leaned against the door. She kept weeping softly. She wrote a note to Lydia that said *Sorry I suck*. Her side work wasn't done. She felt like a big failure.

Joshua picked her up and lay her comfortably in the back seat of his car. He pulled an Oxycontin from his glove box. "I stockpiled them after my last surgery," he joked, and gave her one.

She felt better almost instantly. She sniffled and looked out at the navy western sky.

CHAPTER SIX: BROKEN ANKLE

"It's broken," the doctor said. They had waited in the reception area for a long, long time. Then, they waited for the nurse to arrive for a long, long time. Then, the doctor. Then, the X-Ray results. As they waited, Joshua facilitated rounds of hangman and tic-tac-toe and twenty questions. They giggled through the pain. It was getting very late. Finally, the X-Rays arrived and confirmed what Donna already suspected: her ankle and foot were broken, and she was doomed to a cast for at least six weeks and a brace for even longer.

"You have options," the doctor said. "We can give you crutches to move around in, or a wheelchair if you need one. What is your living situation like? Will you be able to get in and out?"

Donna looked at Joshua. "We're roommates." He stepped in. "I'll take care of her."

"Wonderful," the doctor said, and wrote Donna a prescription for more painkillers. Joshua looked at her and winked. "Things will be hard," the doctor continued. "Try to keep your foot elevated. Sleep with it elevated if you can. Bathing and showering will be tricky. You can bathe and keep it propped on the edge of the tub, or you can shower with it wrapped in plastic. Please be careful getting in and out. We don't want you to hurt yourself even more. Sound good?"

"Sounds good," Donna sighed. She'd be fine with her crutches, but Joshua insisted on wheeling her to the car in a wheelchair.

"At least let me get one photo," he said. "You look so cute and pitiful." Donna held up a skeptical peace sign and let Joshua get his laugh. "Say 'Broken ankle!'"

Donna said it but tried not to chuckle too hard because everything hurt. "You're so extra," she said.

Joshua grinned and he lifted her up, stronger than he looked, and got her into the car. The car clock said 1 a.m.

"Jesus," she said. "I'm sorry. Let's get home."

"Or we could go for a drink," Joshua said. Donna laughed and he followed up, "What? We deserve it."

"Okay, yeah, one drink."

They pulled up to a dark, velvety late-night bar called the Maui Sugar Mill Saloon and got two banana daiquiris in tiki statues. Donna didn't remember much of the night after ordering — she forgot she had taken a painkiller, so the gin went straight to her head.

She woke up late the next day, around eleven, tucked safely into her bed. Joshua left a note:

> *Your boss Lydia came by while you were asleep. I told her what happened and that you are okay but needed a mental health day. Hope that's okay. She understood. Let me know if you need anything and I'll see you tonight.*

Her head hurt and her leg hurt even more so she took another painkiller. She realized it was her first time home during the day without Joshua, since he'd moved in. She felt the urge to snoop around but didn't quite know why. Maybe just for the fun of it? When was the last time she had snooped on someone?

She got on her crutches and hobbled to his door. She hadn't even seen his room since he moved in and wondered what he had done with the place. She sighed deeply and placed her hand on the knob. To her surprise, the door was locked. Upon closer inspection, she noticed the doorknob had been replaced with a locking door that had a small keyhole. When had he done that? And why?

She felt silly even asking the question. He did it to ward off snoopers, which she clearly was. It was unsettling regardless. Did he have something to hide? She pressed her ear to the door to make sure he wasn't home. She couldn't hear anything so checked outside where he usually parked. His car was gone. Carefully, she got on her hands and knees and looked under the door. Strangely, nothing seemed to be touching the floor. From what she could see, there was no bed or dresser or any furniture at all — only a yoga mat coiled up and leaned against the wall. There was also a suitcase, zipped and resting neatly on the ground. That was it. Where were his belongings? Where were his clothes?

Then in the room, she heard a faint rustling. Her heart stopped. He was home. She shuddered in embarrassment, a naughty child caught misbehaving. Mortified, she tried to make a quick decision — the only way out would be to confess to nosing around and apologize. But at the second rustling sound, she second-guessed herself. The noises didn't sound like human footsteps. She kept her ear pressed to the door for some time but couldn't figure it out. Maybe it was a ventilation issue she hadn't noticed before. Or maybe he'd left his window open.

Disturbed, Donna decided to take a bath. It was a fiasco, getting herself in and out. Her foot sat propped on the edge of the tub. She sat there for so long, thinking about Joshua and the doorknob and the rustling, that the water went cold around her. It occurred to her that she had an itch on her calf. She tried to scratch it with the back of a toothbrush but couldn't get it. She mourned that she wouldn't be able to ride her new bicycle and suddenly felt completely alone.

* * *

Lydia was perfectly understanding about the situation. "I turn off my cell for five seconds and all hell breaks loose," she said on the phone. "How long have you been with us now — three months yet?"

"Not quite," Donna said sadly.

"Well, close enough," Lydia said. "We need to get you on the health insurance."

"I'm supposed to have worked ninety days," Donna said.

"You're not going anywhere, are you?" Lydia asked "I'll get it set up on Monday. You should be able to back bill your emergency visit. I feel bad."

"It's not your fault," Donna assured her. "I'm a total klutz."

Lydia promised not to schedule her for any closing shifts until her foot healed. She did continue to work reception, in her boot. Some clients still liked to be walked to their hairdressing chairs with Donna on crutches; others insisted she not get up. She kept making coffees and teas and glasses of champagne, when requested, and hobbling them over.

Before the boot, Donna had never made any tips of her own. With the boot on, she was raking in forty — sometimes fifty! — extra dollars a day.

At the end of the week, Donna asked Lydia what she thought about Joshua during their quick visit.

"Oh, he was a doll," she said. "I don't know what I pictured. But that guy is nice. Thank god you have someone there to take care of you." Donna nodded her head slowly and left it at that. She didn't want to raise any concerns about Joshua — maybe the weirdness was all in her head.

* * *

Interactions with Joshua appeared normal. They kept watching Food Network and filled the time together. The news was increasingly overwhelming. At the start of the new year, 2018 quickly proved to be a mess. Seven people were run over by a truck in San Francisco. A woman tried to bring an emotional support peacock onto a United Airlines flight. And Donald Trump was just unspeakable. The Food Network was easier.

Donna was troubled about the new doorknob but didn't know how to bring it up with Joshua. Surely, he had a right to privacy. But they were friends, so on a personal level she felt a bit left out. What could he have he didn't want her to know about? Was it money? He must know she wouldn't dream of robbing him. And if she did, it would be super obvious. No, it must have been something embarrassing. But what could be embarrassing about him? And why was he ashamed to let her know?

She kept a close eye on the day-to-day and noticed the door wasn't locked while he was home. He moved in and out of it freely. He must only lock it when she would be home without him. So far, that was only that one time. But why go to all the trouble? She wondered. She could just as easily creep in while he was asleep.

Finally, one night over *Barefoot Contessa,* a commercial came on and Donna found the courage to say something. She gulped hard on her glass of wine and said plainly, "Joshua, I want to talk to you about something."

"I do, too," he said, surprising her.

"Oh. Okay." Donna hesitated. "Do you want to go first?"

"I do," he said. "I am not going to pay rent this month. It's only fair. I went above and beyond with your injury. I have taken care of you and made sacrifices to ensure you are comfortable around here. I am happy to do it, but in many ways, it has been like a job, and I don't believe I should pay."

Donna was taken aback but didn't know how to defend herself. "Okay, uh . . ." she began, "that is something I am willing to talk about."

"We are talking about it now," Joshua said. His serious tone took her off guard. She had never seen this side of him before.

"I know."

"The conversation is happening now," he finished. "We're not tabling it."

Donna tried to remember everything she knew about successful communication from her few times in therapy, or in the few psychology classes she took. She remembered "I" statements. But "I" what? She went for it.

"I would like to know more about why you think my leg injury should exempt you from rent."

"I should have known you would be sarcastic," Joshua said. It was the first time Donna had heard him be harsh. She was a little shocked.

"I'm not being sarcastic," Donna said. "Really, I want to know."

"First of all," Joshua said, "I took time out of my evening off to come rescue you. I saved you from thousands of dollars in an ambulance. We didn't get home until almost 3 a.m., at which point you were too drunk to even get yourself in bed. Then the next morning, no offense, you were too hungover to wake up at a reasonable hour and so I had to talk to your boss for you. Since then, it's been a lot of emotional labor."

Donna was horrified. Her face became pink and hot. "Joshua," she said, "I had no idea this was weighing on you."

"It hasn't weighed on me," he argued. "This is all recent. I am telling you before rent is due in February, due to the fact that I will not pay."

"Getting drinks was your idea," she went on. "I didn't drink too much. I was on painkillers."

"Respectfully, you should be responsible for your actions and do not mix medication and alcohol if you know you will have a poor reaction."

"Are you kidding me?" she shot back, then recollected herself. "Pay half the rent."

"Absolutely not," he said. "And this is reasonable. I have been very generous with you."

"Joshua—"

"Donna, as a tenant in this house, I have a right to quiet enjoyment just like you," he said. "And you have not given me that this month with your drama."

"I am trying to understand what drama."

"We can discuss this in court if you want to," Joshua said, pouring another glass of wine. Donna wrinkled her brow. *Court?* She didn't even have him on a proper lease. How would he take her to court?

"I'm okay. Thanks," she said. By now, Ina Garten was back on screen talking about the easiest way to tie up an entire lamb. Donna's eyes were blurring.

"What did you need to ask me?" Joshua said.

"Never mind," Donna said. "Let's just watch the show." They sat in hostile silence for a few moments before Donna got up and hobbled to her room. She closed the door gently, even though she wanted to slam it as hard as she could. Lying in bed, she heard Joshua chuckling at the television, like nothing had happened. He was just gleefully watching Ina Garten on her grandmother's couch, in her grandmother's house, the beautiful cottage he apparently would not pay for this month.

He stayed up late that night and had a great time. It drove her insane. She had to go to the bathroom so badly but was too prideful. She was humiliated thinking of moving past him slowly, awkwardly on her crutches. She peed in an old water bottle and placed it under her bed. She tried to sleep but failed, feeling like her body was being lowered into a pot of boiling water.

* * *

In the morning, with a sense of new energy, she met Joshua in the kitchen. He was pouring himself a cup of coffee. "Good morning," he offered. "Do you want some?"

Donna said yes and stared him down.

"Can I help you?" he asked.

"I'm upset."

"What about? We reached a fair agreement," he said.

"Why did you put a locking doorknob on your door?"

He gave her the coffee and pulled out a chair for her to sit on. He sat beside her. "I have a right to privacy," he said. "You probably saw the lock because you were trying to snoop."

"I wanted to see what you did to her room," Donna said. "I was curious."

"It's not your business," he said calmly.

"It's my house."

"I need you to be more mindful about what you expect of me. We're roommates, not life partners. We have to have boundaries."

"I do have boundaries," she said, "which is why I need you to pay rent this month. I don't owe you any favors."

"Come here," he said. He hastily led her to his bedroom door and threw open the door. It was just as she had seen under the door. There was a yoga mat rolled up and a suitcase packed neatly on the floor. She couldn't see into the closet — the door was closed — but she got the point.

"Where is all the furniture?" she said.

"I didn't want any."

"Where do you sleep?"

"On the floor," Joshua said. "Like the Japanese." Donna gave him a look. "What? It's good for your back."

"Why lock the door then?" she asked.

He softened some. "It's the mental stability I like. Nothing more. I've been in some weird situations in the past and want to protect myself by making boundaries. It's nothing personal against you."

Donna understood, vaguely. "Joshua," she said. "I need to ask you to tell me when you do something like that. Otherwise, I start to wonder. When you make changes to the house, I need you to tell me."

"I will tell you," he said. "I apologize."

She was taken aback by his apology but remembered he was still the person she knew. Even if he refused to pay this month's rent, even if he insisted on locking his door, he was still the sweet, balding gentleman she had met for drinks that night. He was still the person that reminded her of a close cousin.

"Thank you," Donna said. "I appreciate it."

Joshua tried to change the subject. He sipped his coffee and asked how the salon was going. He tried to explain his lack of furniture, how he was just weird like that, and brought up times in the past when he had more stuff that just collected into anxious piles.

Donna was barely listening, though. Her mind was rattled. Since her father left, she had been a loyalist to a fault. She despised Joshua for bringing out this trait. Her happiness began to crack, and she was afraid it was the start of a total break.

* * *

Their connection somehow both grew stronger and faltered at once. The ease with which they once coexisted was gone, but now their relationship required more attention and finesse. Between them, a strange yearning and anxiety grew whenever the other was absent. When Donna got home, she checked if he was home. If he was away, she felt both upset and relieved. Being around him kept her out of her head and in the moment. Late nights silently enjoying the Food Network, being alone together, were replaced by long, emotional conversations. Since Joshua had pushed back about the rent, Donna tried to avoid the next reveal. And with this new fire under the friendship, the two started to share everything, even deeper darknesses of their past. Beyond Joshua's quirks and flaws, his display of trust in Donna as a listener helped the friendship feel secure.

One night, he joined Donna for a cigarette on the front porch — he didn't smoke typically so she gladly bummed him one, open to the extra chat and company. Then, in the special way that only moonlit conversations escalate, the two soon started to talk about love.

"I've been thinking about something you said," Joshua said, "Early on. I believe the very first night we met."

Donna raised her eyebrows and took a quick drag in response, interested to know what had stuck with him.

"About how you always wanted a super dramatic relationship. I told you my relationships tended to err on that side. But one didn't — and that one, in the end, hurt most of all. I thought he'd be the one — maybe we'd even marry. One day I looked up and realized it was over."

Donna had never been close to finding a soulmate and the idea of finding one and then losing him affected her. "Why did it end, then? Did he cheat?" she asked. "What would make it end so suddenly?"

"It wasn't sudden," Joshua said. "That's the thing." He curled his bare toes over the concrete edge of the front step and paused, his face somber and pretty in the late Topanga light. "With this guy, the whole tone was different. Slower, quieter. It was nice. But over time, I learned more and more about why he didn't see me as a fit partner. And tragically, nothing big and bad happened — it was petty grievances he didn't like. Stuff I couldn't change about myself."

Donna put down her cigarette and touched Joshua's shoulder. "You have your idiosyncrasies," she said. "but what's not to like?"

"Like, the way I chewed, for example," he said.

"You do smack sometimes!" Donna laughed.

"It is funny," Joshua said, "but it's also very sad. It's pathetic when you are trying to be yourself with someone and they just decide they don't like you — so much so that they are willing to throw you away." He exhaled. "What am I on about? Here I am jading a young, fresh, single soul like yourself. And for what? Love is fine. Love is good. Everybody wants it. That's what we're all after."

"We'll find it," she said. Joshua squeezed her hand. A wide, gray moth danced against the porch light — there were so few bugs around LA, and even the bugs were beautiful. Donna relished this moment with him, reflecting on how their opposites seemed to fill into one another like coloring in the lines. Sometimes Donna craved Joshua's older wisdom and he seemed to seek her young perspective. But in these patterns, they were constantly back and forth, both understanding and offending one another, stepping on each other's toes, second-guessing. They needed one to complete the other. They had become morbidly codependent.

Donna's foot healed slowly. It seemed time could not slow down anymore. And the activities Donna expected would get easier as she got used to the cast actually became harder because she became impatient and did things half-heartedly. This led to more slips, more falls, fewer nights with her ankle propped up, and more irritation. Joshua tried to help her the entire time, but Donna didn't want much of it. She didn't want him to have any reason to withhold further payments.

One evening she was trying to relax in the bathtub and Joshua accused her of spending too much time in the bathroom. "If we are going to share it, we need to share it," he said. "You spend considerably more time in the bathroom than me," he went on, "and I don't think that's very fair for our rent situation."

Donna cringed and promised to evaluate the time she spent in the bathroom. While the conversation happened, she balanced awkwardly on his shoulder, her towel still on, her body dripping. Mid-conversation, she began her period and blood fell onto the floor. Joshua looked at the small puddle on the ground and just said, "Nice," and left in a huff.

The next day he texted her an apology. It was insensitive, he claimed, especially when she had been looking for a female roommate in the first place. But he ended the text message ominously, stating, *Many details of this arrangement are not what we expected . . .*

Every little thing he said hurt Donna's feelings. She wanted to hurt him, too. When he made plans and didn't invite her, she made a point to put dishes loudly in the cabinet and slam doors. When she didn't invite him to stuff, he wouldn't say a word. Not even a question. It was entirely aggravating.

Finally, the day came for Donna's cast to be removed. When they cut the cast off with a dramatic saw, her pale, feeble leg looked so stupid and vulnerable. Her toenails were long. Her ankle was tiny. She was pasty and hairy. Who knew one could be so self-conscious about a leg? And, it stank.

Drinks? she texted Joshua. She wanted him to meet her and be impressed that she was out of her cast. She wanted him to see her and think, "She's so independent. She didn't even ask me for a ride."

Instead, when she arrived to meet him at Canyon Bistro, she almost couldn't find him. After circling the building a few times, she finally saw him. His head was face down on the table and he was shaking, crying hard.

CHAPTER SEVEN: BEREAVEMENT

His mother had died. She had gone out to the stable in wherever-the-fuck small town she resided in Nevada and took a pistol to her head.

"I bet blood got all over those horses," Joshua cried. "The white horse, Rookie, was my favorite."

Donna didn't know what to say. She had a lot of questions but offered little support. She wanted to know if his mother had struggled with depression, if it was a surprise, if he was traveling to the funeral. Joshua gave vague answers to all of the above and was offended that she didn't offer many condolences.

Finally, she scratched his back and said, "I'm so sorry."

That made Joshua cry harder. He collapsed into her chest for comfort, making her feel like a mother. He felt betrayed, wailing and wondering how she could do this to him. Truthfully, Donna didn't know how anyone could do this to anyone. But certainly it was more than that. Certainly it was beyond doing harm to people. Joshua told Donna his mother had a shadowed past with suicide, so it was probably a necessary reaction to an unendurable pain.

Joshua had his problems, but she imagined he was probably an easy child. She was curious about his mother. She wanted to see photographs of her, and to get inside her head a little bit. She wondered if he had any siblings. Were his parents even together when his dad died? Donna wasn't sure, and after her first tepid reaction to the news, she was afraid to ask further questions.

As Joshua soaked his sleeves with his tears, he got drunk and began to not make sense. Donna tried to soak in more information about where he was from, but he gave vague, gibberish answers. He had one too many. Two too many. Three too many. Then, her mission was just to get him home safe. They paid the check and Donna loaded him up in the car. He could get his in the morning.

Once they pulled up to the house, they sat out front for a few minutes. "I don't know how I'm going to afford this," he cried between sobs. "Any of it."

"Any of what?" Donna asked. "The flights?"

"The funeral," he said. "I'm all she has."

* * *

Donna felt devastated for him. His mother was wiped from the Earth in an instant, and in such a gruesome, disgusting way that disturbed her. She couldn't stop thinking about Rookie's hair, that white horse, and wondering if he was still alive, and wondering if he got splattered with blood. Surely that would stain a white horse.

In any case, she told Joshua to just get through the next few weeks and they could talk about money later. It did put her in a bind. She wasn't exactly raking in bills at the hair salon, but she wasn't destitute. Joshua laid low for a little, as Donna expected, so she decided to do some of the California activities that had brought her here in the first place.

She rode up and down the coast. The experience was lonely and made her wish she had a motorcycle rather than a car. She tried to rent one, but, apparently, she needed a special motorcycle license. Whatever.

So she rolled down her windows and went up the coast in no particular direction. She drove for hours, feeling the air outside getting considerably colder the farther she went north. Still, she kept them rolled down.

There was one point she felt so lonely it occurred to her that she could also shoot herself in a horse stable. She didn't think of it because it was something she actually wanted to do — more so, just knowing she had the ability to do something like that if she ever chose to was liberating. Her fate was under her control, mostly. At one point in the journey, she got out of the car on some dark beach and cried her eyes out. She missed her mom and felt like there was no one to hold her accountable in life besides Joshua. And Joshua had been distant, and Lydia was just a work friend. California had turned out to be so god-awfully depressing. And also beautiful. The beauty was the most depressing part.

She bought a fresh pack of cigarettes and smoked half of them. She called and told her mom this, wanting to connect, but the whole ordeal made her mother furious.

"You're just driving around in the dark by yourself and chain-smoking?" Addie asked. "What the fuck do you want me to say? I'm your mother. Don't do that."

Then Donna was at a small bar on a beach, drinking champagne and calling her mother back again. She told her about Joshua's mom. "Don't ever do that to me," Donna pleaded.

"Donna," Addie said. "I am so sorry for Joshua, but you know very well I would never do that to you, so please, honey, can you get some sleep? You sound drunk and honestly, I'm bordering between concern and anger, okay, honey? Go to bed."

So Donna got a motel room in Santa Maria, the most affordable she could find, and drifted in and out of daydreams in the bath. She fell asleep in a giant, comfy, white robe, swam in the hotel pool and got a brisket sandwich through room service. She felt cathartic. Refreshed.

The bill was enormous.

* * *

"You what?" Joshua asked. "How could you afford that?"

"I put it on a credit card," Donna said. "And I don't use my credit card like, ever."

"No judgment here," Joshua said judgmentally.

"How was your weekend?"

"It was shit considering my mom just shot herself in a stable."

"Sorry."

"I need support right now, Donna," Joshua said.

"You've barely been home!" she contested. "Do you want me to sit around here and wait for you?"

"You could have called."

"And what? Would you have come with me?"

"I can't afford room service!" he shouted.

"So what do you want from me?" Donna pleaded, on the edge of tears. Their companionship was getting more toxic by the day. Donna wanted to flee to her room and slam the door, but she also wanted to commiserate with him and let him know she was there.

Joshua softened and became sensitive. "It turns out no one loved my mom, so I don't have to plan a funeral for her after all," he said. "I'm still going to go, though. We all are."

Aha. There they were. The siblings.

"How many siblings do you have?" she asked, carefully.

"Two," he said. "A brother and a sister."

"And are you . . ."

"The youngest," he said solemnly. "I'm the baby." Donna paused. She wasn't sure what to say. "I know," he said abruptly. "It's surprising because I take care of fucking everyone!"

Then he was drinking again. It was like a flash. There wasn't alcohol and then suddenly there was. He practically poured it down his throat.

"Where do they live?" Donna asked. "Your brother and sister?"

"Not too far," Joshua said. "They both work in Bakersfield." Donna wondered why she had never met them. Why he'd never mentioned them before.

"It will be healing for you all to go to Nevada," Donna said. "Get away for a little bit."

"You just want me out of your hair," Joshua pouted.

"Honestly," Donna laughed. "I do. I'm not totally sure how to talk to you right now."

Joshua laughed through tears. "Thank you for being honest."

They went back to the Food Network that night. It felt like old times, even though they had only known each other for five months. It felt like some compassion was restored. They could laugh through the pain again. They fell asleep on the couch beside each other, Donna nestled into Joshua's armpit. It was nice to feel each other's warmth. Joshua's breath stank a little bit, but in a nice way. In a way that felt like familiarity, like waking up early with family on a holiday. Donna's faded blue hair was tangled into his beard. The bedroom doors were both open. There was a sense of acceptance in the air.

CHAPTER EIGHT: THE HABITAT

When Donna woke up, Joshua was gone. She hadn't heard him leave, so she texted him hoping he was okay. He usually responded quickly. That day, he did not respond. She felt a little worried but assumed a lot was going on in his head.

At this point, Joshua had not paid the rent for two months. That made Donna cringe, but the timeline was somewhat logical. There was the month with the disagreement, then soon after, tragedy struck. Surely, once things settled with his family, he would be back on track. Still, her pantry every week filled less and less with fresh vegetables and more and more with beans and rice and pasta and PB&J's. She didn't want to be dramatic, but she needed filling foods that she could afford.

His door was left open.

This shocked Donna. His door hadn't been open since she'd moved in. She wanted to go in and explore, but it felt like a trap. Maybe he'd set up a camera just to prove a point. "Right when I left my door open, you go in," he would say, snidely.

His room looked like a tiny, dark portal at the end of an unsuspecting vortex. When he was gone, it felt like her grandmother's house again. Unfamiliar but still cozy like home. When he was there, she felt on edge, like she had something to prove. His door was open and the days passed and she stared at it. She wanted so badly to go inside but knew an invasion of privacy could come back to screw her over.

Finally, after four days, she started to notice a smell — like food going bad. Joshua must have had a snack in his room that was rotting. Donna was curious but didn't think it warranted a disruption of privacy. But then the smell got worse and worse. Finally, she couldn't stand it. If he found out she had gone in, she would tell him the truth: there was a smell and she had to stop it.

So, she went in.

It was just as before, with the lack of furniture. And now, there was a lack of a suitcase. He'd obviously brought it with him on his trip. His yoga mat was rolled up and placed neatly in the corner. The floors looked vacuumed and respected.

"It must be in the vents," Donna thought, and prepared to leave. But then she heard a rustling. It was the same rustling she had heard those few months ago, from the inside of the room. It put her on edge. What was the rustling? She inched around, her small feet making the hardwood squeak. She heard the rustling again, and then she heard what sounded like a hiss.

She inched toward the closet hesitantly. As she got closer, the hissing noises got a bit louder, then louder. She began to lightly panic. It was surely a vent that was crooked or a mouse that got trapped in the wall. Still, she didn't like mice and prayed she wouldn't encounter one.

It was nearly pitch black as the lightbulb was out. Ever so lightly, she tapped at the closet door. When she tapped, the rustling and hissing noises went completely silent. She placed her hand on the doorknob, turned it ever so slightly, and let the closet door open a crack.

In the faint, faint sliver of light, she saw what looked like a green-and-black bead. She squinted and focused on the bead. The black part of it moved and moved again. Then, she heard a long, drawn-out hiss. She was looking into the eyes of a snake.

At first, Donna couldn't process what she saw. His face was tiny, his eyes big, his scales a misty, fantastical shade of gray. But what shocked her the most was how his body wrapped and wrapped and wrapped in a never-ending coil.

Behind him, in a clear plastic tote, lay a pile of dead mice. One of the mice was wiggling, its little baby eyes begging for death. But the snake wouldn't kill it. He was looking at the mouse like, "No. I want you to suffer."

His body was as long as the skin Donna had seen, maybe twenty feet long, and thin. He looked hungry, like he hadn't eaten in days. The mice piled up like the food of a picky toddler. He didn't want to eat mice. He was saving himself for something better.

It occurred to Donna that Joshua had piled the mice there before he left — he wanted the snake to be fed during his trip, but he didn't want to tell Donna the snake existed. The snake's eye flickered again onto Donna, almost smiling at her. The weight of the reality that a twenty-foot reptile had been sitting in her grandmother's closet for the past five months settled on her, and she almost vomited up her beans and rice and PB&J and Chardonnay. Taking a deep breath, a chill washed over her. She suddenly felt like she could freeze to death. The snake's eyes stayed on her, unmoving. She wished she were dead. And like a wish come true, she fainted, headfirst, into the closet.

* * *

When she awoke, the snake was measuring her. Outstretched straight as a ruler, from the tip of her head to fifteen feet past her toes. Its eyes were level with her eyes, so when she awoke, they locked gazes immediately. It was like she was waking up to a lover, a lover whom she couldn't trust, a lover who might kill her at any second.

Her body went into autopilot. She quietly and calmly stood up from where she'd fallen. She slowly began to walk back towards the door. As she walked, the snake slowly uncoiled. Once the length of its body was in the bedroom, she closed the door, knowing it would lock shut behind her. She tugged at the knob to make sure.

Then, of all things, she realized she had left her phone in Joshua's room.

* * *

Donna expected a heart-wrenching confrontation. She emailed Joshua to see if he would video chat from her computer. She said she apologized and knew it was a sensitive time, but that it was urgent and she would appreciate it.

He responded instantly. *Any time.*

Her fingers trembled as she waited to dial the call. She wasn't sure what tone to use. Would she mention the snake first or trespassing in his room first? If she mentioned the snake first, it would put him in the wrong. But if he was automatically in the wrong for keeping a snake, then she was in the wrong for entering without permission. People have pet snakes, she told herself to talk herself off the ledge, and they aren't all bad. As she was deliberating, he dialed her. She hesitated briefly, then answered.

"Hi," she said. She looked at her image on the webcam. She looked like a dirty little troll.

"Are you okay?" Joshua said. "What's the matter?" He seemed genuinely concerned. This put Donna at ease a little.

"Joshua," she said. She felt the urge to cry but sucked it back. "Something terrible happened."

"You found him, didn't you?" Joshua said. "I'm so sorry."

Donna gasped. Now a single tear was falling down her face.

"I didn't know how to tell you," Joshua went on. "Especially after you told me your fear that night at dinner. It's so stupid of me, I know."

Donna laughed in frustration. She was angry, humiliated, and had so many questions. "Joshua, I'm really freaked out by snakes," she said. "Why would you do this?"

"I've had him for a long time," Joshua said. "I knew it would be a deal-breaker."

He was right. It probably would have been a deal-breaker. But the real kicker was that he had not been honest. "You should have told me. I'm pissed at you."

"Okay," Joshua said.

"Then on top of it all, I left my *fucking* phone in there! And I locked it! Of fucking course."

But then Joshua was laughing, and in spite of her anger, she wanted to laugh, too. But she held onto her rage and stifled it.

"I want to fucking kick myself for leaving it in there with that monster," she shrieked. "What were you thinking?"

"I don't know," Joshua said. "I don't. I just met you and liked you so much and I didn't . . . know . . . what to say about it."

Donna sniffed.

"Really, Donna, I didn't."

"Is it safe?" she asked.

"Yes."

"And he just eats mice?"

"He eats mice," Joshua said, then laughed. "And little girls named Donna."

"Stop it!" she demanded. "It isn't fucking funny."

"Sorry, sorry," he said. "When I get back, I'll give you a formal introduction. Unless . . ." he trailed off.

"Unless what?"

"Unless you want to kick me out."

Donna paused. She hadn't considered kicking him out, but now that he'd said it, she couldn't help but consider it. What was more than the snake — she needed him to pay rent and not lie to her face.

"Donna?" he asked.

"Sorry," she said. "I'm angry. I'm not throwing you out, but I need to think about some things."

"Okay," was all he said.

The silence was painful. She wanted to change the subject, and fast. "How is your trip?" she asked. "How are your siblings?"

"Somehow worse than I am, if you can imagine," he said. "I've been such a mess."

"You really haven't," Donna said. "I think you've been handling it well. Relatively."

"I'm ready to come home," Joshua said.

"Isn't that weird?" Donna said. "How when you say 'home' you mean here?"

Joshua laughed hesitantly. She laughed, too, even though she had big reservations about their closeness. Suddenly wanting to create a distance between them, she added, "Stay safe," and hung up.

CHAPTER NINE: COLE

For the rest of Joshua's trip, Donna spent as much time outside as possible. She hated being indoors alone with the snake, at least until she could "meet" him properly. She had decided to work on the garden, which had been completely neglected since her arrival. The mint was out of control, and the tomatoes had dried into prunes.

She was a first-timer and didn't want to set the bar too high for herself, so she decided to clean it up and stick to the basics. She wanted to trim what was there, see what shape the plants took, and give the garden a look that someone had at least acknowledged its presence. Rudy left a robust collection of tools behind, so Donna spent some time in the sunlight and got her hands dirty.

She plucked and picked, cut and trimmed, pulled up weeds and raked the soil; her arms became tan and her nose red. She thought about Lydia at the hair salon, how Lydia would cut hair maybe like a gardener would trim a garden. What colors would look nice? What length? An unruly, wilder look appealed to her, so she kept the grasses and the flowers long — the garden was groomed but still had an edge.

It was early spring —after living in Chicago, the concept of winter in Topanga had made her laugh. It had been the warmest winter she'd ever experienced. After picking up seeds from the local dollar store, she planted tomatoes, cucumbers and marigolds. Then in smaller pots, she planted basil, dill, oregano and cilantro. She added some begonias to the window boxes and even got a small azalea bush for Rudy's mosaic pot inside. Taking Polaroids of everything, she hung the photos on the refrigerator — realizing her new gardening hobby brought her immediate pleasure.

Despite her fear and anxiety, there was something sweet about the melancholy Donna faced. There was a snake in her home and she was terrified of it, but his presence made her feel alive again. It gave her feeling back, albeit an unpleasant one, where she had been vacant for several years.

* * *

Joshua had been gone much longer than he expected. In his absence, she met someone.

She didn't meet Cole on purpose. She stumbled upon him, during one of the few evenings she'd taken herself out. It was Lydia's birthday and Lydia convinced her to go join some friends at the bar. When they arrived, Lydia was quickly swept away by a mob of artsy, tattoo-wielding cosmetologists, and Donna felt awkward and left out. She smiled and made nice but wasn't sure what to say to anyone.

He was much taller than she was — gaunt and a little funny looking. He wore a cream-colored button-down and a pair of dark wash Levi's. He had a dark shadow of a beard coming in and wore a sturdy, brown hiking backpack and a pair of black Adidas. Before he spoke, Donna noticed a faint, nice smell of oatmeal coming from him. It reminded her of the soap her mom used.

"Are you here for Lydia's birthday?" he asked.

"I am," she said. "Are you?"

"Yeah," said Cole. "But I don't even know her." Donna didn't laugh, but the silence between them wasn't awkward. It was a friendly silence where a laugh would go. "My friend does," he went on. "He dragged me along." Another long silence, then Donna smiled.

"Can I sit here?" Cole asked.

"Sure," said Donna, moving her backpack out of the chair beside her.

At first, they didn't laugh at each other's jokes. But then, when they realized they didn't find the other funny, they started to laugh hard at each other. Donna was mesmerized by Cole's direct disposition. He spoke confidently with his hands and nodded actively while she talked. He seemed to be completely there, completely present — he stroked his beard when he was perplexed, hummed when he agreed, and said affirmative yeses throughout the conversation. He was the opposite of bland — he was provocative, opinionated and full of ideas. But he also had moments of deep quiet, where she felt him studying her, wanting to understand her. He had never been to Chicago and asked many questions — about more than just the cold weather.

Throughout their conversation, she watched his face. With every expression, she memorized him more. His face quickly imprinted itself in her brain. Then, she felt it. A slow, squeezing feeling in her chest like there was a rope around her heart. It startled her. It was the first remnant of romantic love she had felt in a long time — maybe even ever.

They shut down the bar that night. She drank what he would usually order, shit beer. He drank what she would usually order, Chardonnay. They ordered like that for each other all night. They had everything in the world to chat about, but the momentary lulls were relaxing and the quiet was kind.

They ended up in his apartment, a tiny but well-organized studio. Donna had expected a sticky man cave, but the place was warm and neutral — it smelled like fresh linen. He lit a "crumb cake" scented candle for extra ambiance and they drank a little more and kissed and kissed. An action movie played in the background, its gunshots and car chases and explosions on mute, but occasionally Cole's eyes would wander to it. She found it sweet that he liked that sort of movie. He found it sweet that she didn't.

"What do you like to watch, then?" he asked.

"Cooking shows, mostly," she said, "and HGTV." He laughed.

She spent two nights in a row at Cole's place. She continued to ask if she was overstaying her welcome and he continued to assure her that she was not.

Cole worked in film, but not in an artistic kind of way. He was a cameraman and liked being on set, but unlike many of his production partners, he didn't want to make films of his own. He freelanced, mostly, but had a solid ongoing contract with a children's network in LA. It was simply a job. He was skilled at it and enjoyed it enough. Donna had questions about his passion, but this confused him. He had hobbies and a big heart. What he enjoyed doing the very most was painting, but he humbly didn't consider himself a proper artist.

He showed Donna his work — a still life of a sink full of dirty dishes, a portrait of a family cooking around a campfire. Donna was struck by the realism and precision of Cole's work. The art was pointedly naturalistic, with no abstract twists, but it had a notable depth of feeling — looking at them was like looking into a personal reflection of how he perceived the world.

"It's wild that you don't sell these," she said. "You could be a professional."

Cole didn't understand why a big career-centered quest was so important to Donna. Truthfully, she didn't understand either — especially as she had no interest in it herself — but then prying him for information about his overarching dreams made her wonder if she was asking these questions of herself.

"Maybe it isn't important," she said, and it was like suddenly her world opened. While she always associated dreams with careers, California provided an opportunity for her to tease out the two. Not having a big career dream in Chicago was what made her a perceived failure. But what seemed more sincerely in line with her desires was a situation in which she felt at the center of her world. She wanted to wake up in command — proud and grateful for her space and her relationships. Her lack of interest in branding herself made her feel almost non-millennial. She wanted a career that satisfied her, but what she wanted even more was a life outside of that career.

There, lazing around on Cole's couch and high on pot, Donna thought of that old cliché: she wanted to work to live, not live to work. Why had that been so hard for her to conceive before?

She felt anxious, in the past, about not knowing her "purpose," at least not in the sense that her classmates defined it. She never had much of a social media presence or even a bio that identified her in any sort of way. While her childhood friends grew up to label themselves as "Founder" or "Lead Consultant" or "Wife-Mom Powerhouse," Donna's bios always contained something vague and lighthearted — a Julia Child quote, an ironic hashtag, a wine glass emoji. She found the most pleasure, she was now less afraid to admit, in being luxuriously herself. In that regard, Cole was a perfect match for her.

He enjoyed every day for the seconds that made it up. He had few worries except for minute-to-minute concerns. In his life, he had survived a tragedy. Both of his parents passed in his twenties, and he was now in his thirties, but he felt grateful for the time he'd spent with them. And he didn't just say that, Donna concluded, he really did feel grateful. But thankfully, he wasn't overly sunny. As Donna bitched about her dead father, Cole didn't once correct her or try to convince her to see it from another perspective. He just laughed, listened and let her be.

Donna still hadn't retrieved her phone from Joshua's room. For all she knew, it had been eaten. She was okay with it, though. It was refreshing to be unplugged for a while, and though she checked in on her email occasionally, for a period she was off the grid. When Cole invited her to stay another night, she knew it was time to go home and left her email with him if he wanted to hang out again.

"I'm sure it won't take too long," he said, and flashed a big, geeky smile.

When she returned home at the end of the weekend, she was happy to find a few of her new seeds had sprouted. She watered them and got ready for the week. It was Sunday night, so she hit the grocery store, washed her dirty clothes and packed a few lunches for the week. She couldn't wait to tell Lydia about Cole.

"I'm not surprised," Lydia said the next morning as the girls got ready to open. "You two squirreled away all night long."

"Did you have a good birthday?" Donna asked, grinning.

"Oh yeah," Lydia said. "But I'm still feeling it today. Two days after. Oh, don't forget, I'm leaving town this weekend for my friend's wedding. Shop's closed Friday and Monday."

"Wow," Donna said. "I did forget." Her mind stirred with possibilities. She had never had two paid days off in her life.

Excited by the possibilities, she contacted Cole, and after some fast deliberating, they decided to be wild and free and take an impromptu vacation to San Francisco. Neither of them had been and they wanted to go somewhere new. Donna hadn't been on vacation since her childhood when her father was still around. And even then, they didn't go to places like San Francisco. They went to places with kitschy coconut shell bras and fake Mexican food. After vacations, Donna was always sunburnt. Now that she lived in LA, she got a healthy dose of sun all year round. She'd mix it up in the rainier and more melancholic scene of San Francisco.

* * *

Donna drove up the coast with Cole in the passenger seat playing DJ, his feet propped up on the dash and his hand on

Donna's knee. He looked like a floppy monkey. On the way, they stopped at a trashy motel and made love, pretending to have a scandalous and shallow affair, but neither of their performances was convincing. They called each other by the wrong name and wore garbage-looking undergarments. They experimented with sex toys. Donna said she liked it rough, so Cole gave Donna one hard spark and awkwardly stammered, "You're a whore," and they descended into laughter and resolved, instead, to comfy, cozy lovemaking.

When it was over, Donna lay on her back and breathed heavily in exhaustion. Staring at the ceiling, she thought about how Cole was so new but felt so right. He didn't feel like a stranger but had hundreds of question marks Donna couldn't wait to learn.

When they got to San Francisco, they both found it a little overstimulating. They had no good local recs and ended up in a crazed tourist trap. Still, they got drunk on Irish coffees at the Buena Vista and took some Polaroids of each other flipping the bird at the Golden Gate Bridge. It was nice to be with each other and by each other, their pinkies linked the whole three days as they hiked breathlessly, high as kites, through the hilly streets.

After sipping tequila sodas in the Castro, Donna realized that in being off the grid she hadn't checked in with Addie for a while. She used Cole's phone to call her up.

"I was scared to death," Addie said. "What twenty-something doesn't even update her Instagram?"

"I'm fine," Donna said. She told her mom her phone was locked away but didn't mention the snake. She also told her about Cole, but Addie was wary about his age.

"It's not because he's that much older than you," her mother rationalized. "It's because I haven't accepted that you are so old."

Donna sighed and promised she could meet him soon. She felt a level of pain, though, that she would never meet his parents. She felt less pain, but did bitterly acknowledge that he would never meet her father. She guessed it didn't matter.

When they were on the way home, Donna felt a sense of dread. She knew the days of crashing at his place and taking impromptu vacations were over. She wanted to invite him to her house, but it didn't feel right. She was preoccupied with the snake and wanted to at least tell Joshua about her boyfriend before having him stay the night.

She told Cole it was the end of their extravaganza, for a little while. When they pulled up back home, they had a soft but long goodbye. It felt weird separating from him.

"I know I can't see you every second," he said. "As much as I want to."

Donna grinned. The funny thing, to her, was that she knew he wasn't a clingy person. But that's just how well they matched. Like a pair of warm woolly socks.

When Donna walked into her home, it smelled worse than ever. Then, she realized Joshua's door was open. He was home.

CHAPTER TEN: HOMECOMING

He was in the shower, and showering very quietly. His presence instantly put her on edge. Every time the soap slid or a shampoo bottle was set down, she would jump. For some reason, she felt like he was mad at her. There was a dark atmosphere plaguing the home. She heard him sigh heavily and was certain it was because of her. When the water stopped, it felt like an eternity for him to get dressed. She pretended to busy herself, to act like she didn't care if he was home or not.

"Look who it is," he said when he walked into the living area. "Where were you?"

"I took a trip," said Donna. She didn't know why she was scared to tell him about Cole.

"I expected to find you at home," Joshua said. "I can't believe you were exploring the country without your phone." He nodded to her phone on the kitchen counter. "I plugged it in for you."

"Thanks," Donna said. She bit her lip.

"You okay?" he asked.

"Yeah. I'm okay." She wanted to gush with him, tell him everything. "I'm just a bit tired."

"Okay. Me too."

There was a long, long pause.

"Do you want to watch TV?" he asked.

"No. I'm sorry, I'm just—"

"You don't have to explain," he said. "We're cool."

He went to his room and closed the door. We're cool? Donna wondered. Why wouldn't they be cool? But for a second she felt she wielded a power. A power that she could be mad about the snake and thus he had to grovel for forgiveness. For once, maybe, she could have the upper hand.

* * *

The next day, Joshua announced he would be working from home now. "I'll try not to trouble you when I'm here," he said. "It's mostly just computer bullshit." To be honest, Donna didn't even understand what field Joshua was in, but whatever it was, it sounded immensely boring. She thought his job was creative, working on user experience and branding. He told her no — it was more like site functionality and speed. Yawnfest. "It's going to be so weird going back to work since my mom passed," he said. "I'm lucky they're letting me work from home. Otherwise, I don't know what I would do."

Donna resisted rolling her eyes. She didn't look forward to him being home so much more. Since his leaving, her heart had not grown fonder for him. When he was around, she felt like she had an infection, like a cold, that she couldn't shake. The living arrangement was fine. He wasn't awful, but the atmosphere was increasingly off-putting. Every little thing he did annoyed her, and even when he cleaned up the smell — she realized it was the smell of dead mice — the stench of Joshua and his negative energy continued to waft through the air.

On top of the negative energy, the stench coming from Joshua's room came back even worse than before. His overall housekeeping capabilities withered. Every day that he worked from home, he left more dishes in the sink, more coffee grounds on the counter, and wet footprints in the hallways. Everything was a noisy fiasco. His every sound amplified in Donna's ears as if it were coming through a megaphone. Objects were constantly falling out of the closet in his room and he would curse, and he got clumsier and started to trip around. She wanted to give him the benefit of the doubt — his mom had passed away, distance between them disrupted their rhythm, she was preoccupied with Cole, and on and on — but still, she couldn't ignore her growing unease.

By this point, Donna had been in California for almost six months. Besides the broken ankle, she had never called off work. She was never late, and clients remarked frequently on her poise and friendliness. It seemed Donna was becoming increasingly busy as Joshua became less busy. His laziness stood out to her and she couldn't ignore it. One morning over coffee, she confronted him. "Can you do more around the house?" she said. "Things are slipping and there's only so much I can do."

He seemed mortified. "I've been so out of it, hon," he said. Then he said, "I miss you," which wildly irritated Donna.

"Why do you miss me?" she barked. "You see me every day and we barely speak."

"That's what I mean," said Joshua. "It's all business all the time, all work all this and that. I wanna just unwind one night and talk."

"You know where to find me," Donna replied coldly.

"Can't we go out?"

Donna checked her watch. She was running late. "Sure," she said. "Tonight?"

"Eight?"

"That's too late for me. Can't we go right after work?"

"What do you have going on?" Joshua pouted.

"Cole," she said. "I have Cole going on."

"Ah," said Joshua. "I knew you would get a boyfriend eventually."

The way Joshua spat out the word "boyfriend" made Donna's hair stand on end. It was so irritating, but she ignored his tone. "Is six okay?" she asked.

Joshua agreed. "And the answer is yes."

"What?"

"Yes, I can do more. I've been a mess. I'm sorry."

"And what about the rent?" Donna added sharply.

"I'll have it printed today." Good. She felt like she had won. "I'm trying, Donna."

When she was just about to exit the door, he asked, "Do you have laundry that needs to be done? I can get on it when I'm home today."

Donna felt a wave of relief. Maybe all her annoyance was built up in her head. Maybe she just wasn't spending enough time with Joshua, and her grief was a symptom of the issue. "That would be great," she admitted. "My door is open."

* * *

At 5:45, Donna waited at Canyon Bistro, where she and Joshua had first met. She ordered shrimp and garlic bread to share, along with a bottle of dry rosé. The same waiter served her as usual. "You two are so funny together," she commented. "How is the living situation going?"

"We're still going out for drinks, so I guess it's okay," Donna said.

"Cheers to that," the waiter said. "Let me know if you need anything else."

As Donna was waiting, Cole texted to see if they could get together. *Me + You = Fritos and Bean Dip Now*, he said.

Lol. Can we meet later? she said. *I have plans with Joshua.*

I'd love to meet him, Cole said.

Donna debated. She was at a small table. Joshua was running behind. Thinking Cole could help ease some of the tension, she decided to invite him. *Canyon Bistro. Join us?*

Perfect, he said. *I'm just down the street.*

Cole arrived within minutes and sat in Joshua's usual chair. He ordered an IPA and picked at the shrimp plate. When Joshua arrived, he was polite and casual. He asked the server if they could move to a bigger table and poured himself a glass of the rosé. "That's the best one so far," he said.

For a while, things seemed to go well. Then, things took a turn for the worse.

Each of the three embarked on a third glass, which was a mistake. The trio should have ended the occasion after some pleasantries and light conversation. It was when the deeper topics came out, specifically about their families, that the mood shifted. It was something that could have united them — they were a dead parents club. Still, each of them had wildly different hot takes: Cole was at peace, albeit melancholy, that his parents' life courses had ended. Donna was withdrawn and sharp about her absent-then-dead father. Joshua was an open, fresh wound that was ready to bleed.

Donna had mentioned to Cole what happened to Joshua's mother. But after a few drinks, Cole was a little too interested in the tragedy. He was unabashedly asking questions, curiously running his fingers through his beard, nodding his head profusely. In the beginning, Joshua was an open book.

"She was depressed for as long as I can remember," he said, "but not violently so. She was a small, delicate woman. I can't even imagine her holding a gun — that's the most disturbing thing."

Although Joshua's tone was stable, Donna was getting restless and she could tell that he was a hissing line of dynamite, but Cole kept going. "Did she always have a gun?"

"Sure," Joshua said. "She lived on a farm — it wasn't an assault rifle. It was a handgun, a pistol."

"So was she one of those pro-gun people?" Cole pried.

"What does it matter?" Joshua asked. "Does it make you feel less sorry for me if she was?"

"I was just curious," Cole asked. "I know there are many responsible gun owners, but I wonder if — you know — this could have been prevented?"

Joshua immediately tensed up. He blurted mockingly, "It could have been prevented." This shut Cole down.

* * *

Against her better judgment, Donna invited Cole back to her place to see the house. He was dying to see inside and wasn't disappointed. "You must think my studio is so sloppy," he said. Soon after they got home, Joshua slinked into his room without saying a word. It was obvious he was still annoyed from the conversation at dinner, but Donna chose to let it go. Cole was still mostly oblivious to the level of tension — he didn't have too much backstory to Joshua and Donna's dynamic anyway — and asked if he could stay the night.

How could Donna say no? He was her boyfriend. He was obviously welcome and besides — it was her fucking house. She was sick of feeling inched out by Joshua. She opted to make the best of it and have some fun. She made Cole a whiskey sour and they watched an episode of *Barefoot Contessa*.

Before bedtime, they were in the bathroom, brushing their teeth. They were a little tipsy, talking loudly, their hair falling into their faces after a long night. Donna was in her underwear, getting the shower going, steam filling the bathroom like a botanical garden. One fern sat on the windowsill, drinking the humidity.

Cole thought the fern was cute and said he always wanted to have a daughter named Fern. "Just a stupid fantasy I had when I was younger," he laughed.

"It isn't stupid," Donna replied. "It's nice to know someone besides me named their fantasy kids." They stepped into the shower, and she rinsed her face off in the water. "Do you really want to have kids?" she asked.

"I don't know," Cole said. "It's funny. The thought of having kids when you're younger is so different from when you are at an actual child-having age," he said. "And when you're actually in love."

Donna knew she loved him, but it was the first time it was said. "You're in love?" she asked as she washed off his back.

"Of course I am," he said, and grinned.

She thought about the strangeness of that phrase: of course. It was something people said so often, and that she said so often, but the connotation of it was always less than what it meant. "Of course" literally means "on the course," as if it were saying, "There is no doubt that this would be true in the progress of our lives." The fact that Cole said his love for Donna was on the course made her heart burst. And there he was — spare, awkward-looking with his clothes that didn't seem to fit him properly, but she didn't mind. He always looked like he was about to go for a hike. His dark, clean denim was out of style. And there was something emo about him even though he was in his early thirties. His green eyes looked like raisins, his eyebrows like bushes.

"I love you, too," Donna said, and admired their bodies in the mirror. They didn't seem to fit together. When they kissed, their teeth clanked. When they hugged, their ribs pushed against one another in an almost painful collision. It was painful because they hugged so hard. They met and began to hug hard as naturally as a reflex.

She was basking in this: the love and the steam and the feeling that there was someone there who she didn't want to leave, and there was a loud banging on the door.

Goosebumps covered her skin.

"Joshua?" she asked.

"You're being so *fucking* loud," Joshua shouted in a sharp tone she didn't anticipate.

"Sorry," she said, and giggled instinctively.

"Is that funny?" Joshua demanded.

Donna didn't know what to say. She and Cole made puzzled eye contact and Cole sucked in through his teeth. Donna stopped the shower and went into the hall to speak to Joshua.

"This is our shared bathroom," Joshua said. "Your business is your business, but I don't feel comfortable with random people using the shower while I'm home."

"He isn't a random person. He's my boyfriend."

"He's random to me," Joshua said. "How would you feel?"

"You mean if you found someone to date?"

"You just met him," Joshua persisted. "It's casual sex and I am not comfortable listening to it."

His words stung Donna. She didn't know what to say. All she could spit out was, "Then use headphones."

She slammed the door in Joshua's face. The romantic moment was ruined. And worst of all, Joshua had got in her head. She looked at Cole, sweet Cole, the man she thought she knew better than anyone even in the short amount of time she had known him. He was standing frozen wrapped in a towel, his skinny legs looking like a boy's beneath the cotton.

"I feel like we just got in trouble by Dad," Cole said. He shrugged his shoulders up to his ears like a giggle. Donna didn't think it was funny.

"Were we being that loud?" she frowned.

"Donna, no," Cole contested. "You're a grown woman. There's no reason why you shouldn't be allowed to have a guy in your shower, in the house that you own."

"You're right." Donna sighed. "He just makes me so *mad*."

"He's going through a lot," Cole said. "Maybe it's just a season."

"It's a fucked-up season," Donna said. She tossed her toothbrush in the cup and started to stomp to her room, her hair still dirty. She picked up a brush and started to violently comb out the tangles.

"You don't want to finish your shower?" Cole asked.

"I'll do it in the morning," Donna said. "I think you should go home."

"Really? Now?" Cole said. "I just got here."

"Cole," Donna said.

"Aw, come on. I want to spend some time together." Cole gave a little smile.

"She said she thinks you should go home," Joshua said from the next room. Donna's heart sank. "Do what she says or we're gonna have a problem."

"Donna, do you want me to leave?" Cole asked. The romantic moment was deflated.

"I don't know," Donna said. "Yes? No? Not because I don't want you here, just because the vibe is . . . terrible." She glanced at Joshua.

"So we have one person who doesn't know what she wants," Joshua started, "and another who doesn't know how to respect boundaries." He came into the doorway, his short body looking somehow large and scary. He looked at Cole, "I think that's your cue to get the fuck out."

"Joshua!" Donna demanded. She wanted to lunge at him, throw her hairbrush at him. Having a dead mom doesn't give you a pass to be an asshole, she rationalized. He was ruining her night.

Joshua was still viciously babbling on. "You said it. The vibes are off and I don't want him here." Donna's heart was racing. She was so embarrassed. "I have a right to exist peacefully, Donna," Joshua reminded her.

"Fine," she caved. "Cole, I think it's time for you to go," she said. "I'll call you." Cole looked exasperated and confused. He left in a hurry and left his small overnight bag in Donna's room. Seeing it made her eyes watery. There were his pajamas and a clean outfit for his job tomorrow. He had brought the bag to her house to spend the evening with her, and sleep beside her. She was shaking in fury. She hated Joshua. She hated everything about him.

CHAPTER ELEVEN: THE LEASE

Joshua did Donna's laundry, just as he promised. But when she was in the salon, she noticed a strange, lingering stench that was all too familiar: the smell of Joshua's stuff at home. It disgusted her. It smelled like unwashed bodies. She didn't understand why Joshua's scent had gotten so bad. Did his mother's death mean he was not taking care of himself like he used to? Or did he always have bad hygiene to begin with. She knew he showered quite regularly, but she was beginning to question if he used soap. And if he did use soap, maybe it was the smell of his clothes that was so off-putting.

She couldn't put her finger on the cause of the issue. Was it mildew? Body odor? She didn't know why, but she began to associate the issue with the snake.

For all Donna knew, the snake continued to thrive in the closet, but it hadn't been mentioned since their initial phone call about it. She concluded the snake was to blame for the smell in the apartment, the smell that lingered on her clothes.

At the salon, she felt immensely self-conscious. When she spoke, she barely looked anyone in the eye. She felt she was pulsing this bizarre aroma throughout the room. Every time she blinked, she pictured snakes and mice and Joshua. She didn't know which he was yet — a snake or a rat.

Whatever her clothes smelled of, even though she couldn't put her finger on it for certain, she knew one thing: they smelled of revenge.

* * *

"I'm going to have you sign a lease," Donna announced. It was a Saturday, two days after the shower fiasco. Joshua still hadn't printed the promised rent check. "I need you to pay rent and I need you to pay it on time. And I need you to deal with the smell *now*."

She was impressed by her own professionalism. She was certain Joshua would accommodate her orders, so she left zero room for discussion. Instead, Joshua pretended he didn't even notice her walk into the room.

"Did you hear me?" she asked.

"Yep," he said, and exited through the side door.

Later that afternoon, Joshua returned confidently, through the side door again, and he was carrying a mini-fridge. He went to his bedroom door, unlocked it, shut it, placed the mini-fridge inside, exited the door, locked it again, and went back out through the side door.

An hour after that, he returned with groceries. He walked them confidently to his bedroom door, unlocked it, shut it, and took the groceries in. He did not make another peep for the rest of the day. Donna sat on the couch the entire time and stared at his door. She was seething. She wasn't answering calls or texts, and she and Cole had barely spoken since the shower episode nights before. She felt humiliated and didn't know what to say to him, even when he texted to make sure she was okay.

Her plan was to confront Joshua, for real this time, about his behavior around and regarding the apartment. She planned to make him sign a lease, and she would have the lease notarized with both parties present. Then, she would show off her new landlordship to Cole. He would be proud of her that she took her life into her own hands.

But, like most things with Joshua, nothing went according to plan.

"Joshua." She knocked. "I need to speak to you."

Unusually, it was raining outside. Drops hit the window pane as fast as the hands of an audience at a pep rally, clapping. The room was dark. Donna had been too lazy to turn the lights on as the evening went on. She was simply existing in her anxiety, her dark thoughts, the rage that Joshua had the wherewithal to completely ignore her, his friend, and go off and purchase a mini-fridge. She was in the dark, lightning striking, anxiety wrenching her stomach, thinking about the coffees and the eggs and the sticks of butter they shared. That was over. And the television — the Ina Garten — if he had his own fridge, then he wasn't allowed to watch the TV. Because that was hers. And it wasn't fair.

And on top of everything, *everything*! She didn't even want him eating in the bedroom to begin with. Because she was the owner, so what she said was supposed to go, and her grandmother never ate in there — couldn't Joshua have any fucking respect — and the food in the bedroom certainly wouldn't make the putrid smell any better.

"Joshua." She knocked again. He was still ignoring her. She didn't even hear him move inside, couldn't even make out the sound of a breath. She heard vague hissing. It was like the snake was guarding him. The snake most certainly had access to Joshua's food, Donna imagined. To him, she was less than a reptile. "Joshua!" she said, nearly screaming this time.

"Come in, Donna," said Joshua. She heard a faint crawl, then the click of a door unlocking. When she opened the door, Joshua was in a comfy heap on the ground. He had a massive berry-colored quilt wrapped around him, and he looked like a small dog inside it. "The rain is nice, isn't it?" he asked. "Rare."

"I don't like it," snapped Donna. "I haven't had the best day."

"You don't like the rain?" he asked.

"I don't know whether I like or don't like the rain," Donna responded. "To me, it doesn't matter." She bit hard into her lip. She knew the ends of her faded turquoise hair looked frazzled and unkempt. The color had become a light, sickly green. She felt like a teenager who was losing her mind.

Joshua flipped on the light. Before, they had been sitting in the dark. When the light went on, Donna noticed Joshua had a black eye.

"What the fuck?" she asked.

"I know," Joshua said. "I've been hiding it from you."

"What happened?" Donna asked, suddenly dropping her agenda.

"Just some street thing," Joshua said. "Outside the grocery store. The guy wanted money, I didn't have it, he really wanted money, I didn't have it. You see where this is going."

"Did you call the cops?" Donna asked.

"No."

"Why didn't you call me?" she wanted to know.

"We haven't been clicking," Joshua said, and Donna turned away from him. His every word sounded like bullshit — her hypothesis was either that he'd pissed somebody off and gotten punched or done it to himself for some twisted sympathy. Both versions of the story annoyed her equally. She wanted so badly to pity him. His mom died, and he had allegedly been mugged. But all the bad events that happened to him only increased her resentment. She wondered if that made her selfish. Or jealous, wishing bad things would only happen to her. And for some reason she was still upset he didn't tell her about these kinds of things as they happened, if they were even real. That's what makes a partnership, isn't it? Sharing? They shared a home, why didn't they share everything else? Donna knew her obsessive watch on Joshua was growing to be more and more irrational, but she couldn't stop it — her thoughts about him swung like a pendulum with the weight of a giant boulder.

Though she hated to admit it, Donna always had a sense of codependency with her living partners. She blamed it on the aloofness of her father. It's why she was so close with her mom — it's why she stuck around with Otto too long. It's why she happily nestled into a comfortability with Cole. She was a sucker for immediate trust and she was patient — she didn't mind a little wrestling in her relationships. But when things got out of control, the stress constricted her.

"I know we haven't been clicking, Josh," she said.

"When have I ever gone by Josh?"

She ignored this. "Just listen. I know we haven't been clicking, but I still care about you and I expect to know what goes on," she said.

"You don't tell me anything either," said Joshua. "You didn't even tell me about Cole. I had to find out in some weird roundabout way of suddenly sharing a meal with someone on the evening we were supposed to be hanging out."

"My phone was locked in your room with your goddamn snake for days!" she shouted.

"Were you impatiently waiting for me here?" Joshua asked. "Because I was putting out FIRES in my FAMILY who has shockingly lost our MOTHER." As he raised his voice, something in his throat grumbled. He sounded like a monster. Seeing him like that, in the sickly light of the fan that had two of the three bulbs out, scared Donna. There was a shadow cast on the side of his face that wasn't beaten up. So next to one another, the two eyes looked equally dark. One was repulsive. The other was oddly mysterious.

Donna thought the two eyes — repulsive and mysterious — represented both sides of Joshua. On one side of him, there was the smelly, snake-owning man whose mother shot herself in the stable. On the other side of him, there was someone who withheld information, kept his room locked tight, and only used the side door.

"I have been patient," Donna said. "So patient," she added, "that I have barely asked you for rent when it is due even though that was our agreement."

"We didn't have an agreement," Joshua replied, coldly.

"What are you talking about?" Donna asked.

"Did you do any paperwork?" Joshua said.

"No."

"Did you record any of our conversations?"

"No."

"I guess we're at a loss, then." Joshua turned out toward the uncharacteristic rain. The shadow moved from the clean side of his face to the bruised side. Now that half of his face was beneath two levels of darkness. The other half was beautiful, and Donna could only see his profile.

"Why are we at a loss, Josh?" she asked.

"Well, we're at a loss because," Joshua paused and laughed darkly to himself. "We're at a loss because I've lived in this house for over six months. And that makes me a legal tenant."

"What do you mean?"

"I mean, I have rights, *baby*," he said. "As many rights as you." Then he got closer and whispered, "And I don't owe you shit. Not now and not ever."

She wanted to throw her fist at him. She wanted to make his single black eye a double. The resentment she held toward how everything had gone wrong for him turned to rage. Why did he get to have a dead mother? Why did he get to have a black eye? Everything that could induce pity toward him from other people made Donna seethe. She was aghast.

"I want to beat your other eye right out of the back of your head," she said. "Just hammer it in so hard it pops through the other side. You pretentious fuck."

"Donna, please." He was calm.

"Take care of the smell!" she screamed. "It smells like shit!" She stomped to the outside of his door and slammed it, knowing it would lock behind her. "And do me a favor and lock yourself in there forever!" She added. "With your stupid fucking fridge! And your mother fucking python!"

She leaned on his door and breathed heavily. She jiggled aggressively at the knob. She didn't know if she was checking to see that it was locked or if she was wanting to add more curses and insults. In any case, steaming tears began to roll down her face. Her chest felt both empty and occupied by grief. She was heavy and full and hollow and barren.

* * *

She was tempted to run away to Cole's but also wanted to stand her ground. So for the next few hours, Donna and Joshua existed in her grandmother's house in a hostage posture. They held themselves hostage. They each refused to be the first to leave. She was too ashamed to call Cole. She missed him to death but didn't want to call him in a time of crisis, and she felt like she introduced nothing but drama to his simple, contented life. She wanted their relationship to be peaceful, to be able to call him just to say hello and that she was thinking of him. One day. Soon. But not today. She couldn't fake shit — she was outraged.

So instead she called her mother. She wanted to convey everything bad that was happening without revealing Joshua's threats. This was for a couple of reasons. One, she didn't want her mother to completely distrust Joshua. What if she decided to get over it and be his friend again? He was in mourning — everyone handles grief differently. But she knew this was a dangerous benefit of the doubt that could screw her. Two, she didn't want to signal alarm bells that she was unsafe. Or that her grandmother's house was in jeopardy. Or that she had screwed everything up by not taking any legal precautions.

Her mom didn't understand the point.

"Then what?" she asked.

"A snake, Mom. He has a snake."

"Well, does he take care of it?" Addie wanted to know. "I dated a guy once, you know, who had a snake. Didn't I tell you that?"

"He didn't tell me about it, Mom," Donna said.

"Sometimes people withhold information," Addie rationalized. "And it hurts, and we have to have a moment of reckoning, and then if the friendship is worth it — move on."

The advice was helpful, if only it weren't completely inapplicable.

"You wanted a roommate," Addie kept going. "Does he treat you well? Does he pay his rent? Remember this was *your* idea. Pick your fights wisely and move on."

Donna froze. The whole reason she had a roommate is because she needed someone to pay rent. But now he wasn't doing that. And not only was he not doing that, but he was also not giving her any kind of emotional fulfillment or bond. Tonight, they were no longer friends. They weren't even frenemies. They were arch-nemeses.

Addie kept talking and talking. "And he helped you when you had a broken ankle . . ." By now, Donna wasn't responding or even listening, but her mother didn't notice. It was a Saturday night and she was home having wine and feeling happy to give her grown daughter advice. She just wanted to feel useful. So Donna let her continue to talk, and she gave the occasional *hmm* and *mmm* for verbal confirmation. But while she listened to her, she was making a list — as seasoned receptionists are wont to do — and the list was called "Alarm Signals."

CHAPTER TWELVE: ALARM SIGNALS

Donna and Joshua existed in a sort of sub-universe, where they were roommates who actively avoided one another. They did stay in the same room at the same time. It seemed like he was always home, staking his post, marking his territory. He even continued to work at home, which was infuriating. By the end of the week, Donna would feel personally affronted that she spent every day at the salon while he spent every day at her grandmother's house. She began to develop sentimental associations with her grandmother, her grandmother whom she barely knew, creating associations she had never had.

She invented fake memories of a childhood where she spent weeks during the summer there. She looked through boxes of her grandmother's personal treasures and thought stuff like, "This is so like her." There were chests full of well-kept nightgowns, vintage hat boxes and powdery glass perfume bottles. She was floating in a sentimental, gorgeous, alternate reality where this senior woman in her family was important to her and taught her life advice.

She finally called Cole. She called on a day when she did just want to tell him hello, but that quickly evolved into other topics. He wanted to know why she had been so distant.

She also wanted to know why he had been so distant. They concluded that they were both embarrassed and needed to keep one another at arm's length as a way of self-protection. Joshua had disoriented them and put their relationship into perspective. Were they moving too quickly? Were they little more than random people to one another?

Donna became consumed by what Joshua was doing and thinking. The sounds on the other side of his door intrigued her. She missed the nights of ease, even though they had only lasted a few sweet months, of having someone to talk to and spend time with. To disassociate, she convinced herself this was a phase. He would pay her rent before she knew it — she had to promise herself that for her sanity — and they would laugh about these weird times. Every relationship had its waves, she told herself, and to wade for too long in anxiety was dangerous. Surely, Joshua knew this because he was older than her. He must be wise, experienced in human interactions. Surely, he knew how to let the negative energy go. As did she. She wanted to sit on a patio with him and drink Chardonnay and eat gouda and salami and watch the California sunset.

Since her falling out of friendship with Joshua and falling in love with melancholy Cole, her world was filled with rain and more rain. Physically and emotionally.

Due to Donna's preoccupations, the garden looked bad. So bad, in fact, that some of the plants looked like skeletons. Donna was certainly disheartened by them. They were like bony corpses crawling out of a graveyard.

"I worked so hard on them," she rationalized, but Cole made a sound point.

"But did you keep up with them?"

"I've had a lot going on," Donna said, a little defensively.

"Well, I think it's partially that," said Cole, "but also partially — that I don't think anything can grow out here." They were standing in the front yard beneath the trees. "Look at all the shadows," he said. "There's not enough light. I find it hard to believe your grandmother gardened out here at all."

"That's the weird thing," said Donna. "The light in the backyard is great."

She took him around back. It only took him a few seconds before he announced his conclusion.

"When she died, or even right before, someone must have moved the garden boxes," he said.

"What?" she asked.

"Those six squares. Those are garden boxes. She grew plants out here."

"That doesn't make any sense," Donna said. "No one has been here. Why would someone move them?"

"Maybe they needed to use the backyard for something else. Was there any construction taking place?" he brainstormed.

"Not that I know of," Donna said. "And besides, wouldn't we see marks from that too?"

"Interesting point." He was walking around the backyard trying to decipher what could have happened back there.

"Do you know if she used this yard for anything else?" he asked.

"No," Donna said. "I don't know. But another weird thing is that . . ." She laughed to herself. She remembered the first time she and her mom drove up and saw the place, and she was struck by the weird backyard. She went on, "Another weird thing is that there was a door attached to the side of the house that looked like, super not right."

"What do you mean?"

"Well, it's still here!" Donna said. "Look at this." She led Cole to the side of the house with the weird side door. "The whole house was like, color-coordinated and immaculate. Then there was this weird fucking side door. I just felt like it was so out of place."

"What did she die of?" Cole wanted to know.

"She had dementia," Donna said. "It started with a brain tumor."

"Well, she could have done some strange things to the house when dementia set in," said Cole.

"Maybe . . ." said Donna. But the door contradicted everything she had learned her grandmother to be — self-assured and nostalgic. The shabby door reminded her of haphazard people, people without taste. If anything, the door reminded her of Joshua.

CHAPTER THIRTEEN: RUDY

Cole's evaluation of the backyard made Donna want to learn more about her deceased grandmother. She went to the grocery store and bought a special binder for her findings. For the front of the binder, she purchased a large bundle of page covers. Fittingly, the binder she purchased was turquoise. For the supplies that would go inside, monochrome rose-gold paper clips and page labels. And for the front cover, she pulled a black-and-white photo of her grandmother in the glory days. In the photo, she was wearing a belted, V-neck, A-line dress with heels and a large flower behind her ears. She was smiling, standing on a small bridge. Donna wasn't sure where the bridge was, but it looked serene.

She called the women in her family, many of which she'd barely spoken to before. Sadly, for Donna, it seemed like many of the family members hadn't known Donna's grandmother so well. But ultimately, Donna gathered, Rudy was supremely introverted and difficult to get to know. "She *was* friendly," Addie had rationalized, "but she was a little, how do you put it, removed."

Friendly and removed. Donna thought the description sounded a bit like herself. But if Rudy was anything like

Donna, Donna knew the coldness was never intentional. It was usually a byproduct of personal insecurities.

"She kept a lot of sentimental objects," one of the cousins said. "Haven't you been able to go through her stuff?"

"That's just it," Donna said. "She has beautiful stuff, but I'm still left with her taste and not much else about her."

"Well, she did have impeccable taste!" her aunt interjected. "She always dressed to the nines, even when she first started going to chemo."

"And then what?" Donna wanted to know.

"And then, you know, she suddenly just . . . didn't anymore."

"That's interesting."

"Well what do you expect, Donna? She was very sick."

"No, I know. I know."

Donna imagined her own health deteriorating. She thought about what she would dress like, how people would describe her. Would she be the removed yet friendly woman who fell apart? Most of all, the interviews regarding her grandmother made Donna wish most of all for resilience. She wanted to be resilient to everything — disease, change. She wanted to be herself, always.

Then, Donna finally connected with her Aunt Sheeba, who was only a short drive to Thousand Oaks. And the call with Aunt Sheeba changed everything.

* * *

Technically, Aunt Sheeba was Donna's great aunt, her grandmother's sister, and though she was older than Rudy, she was in better health. The drive from Topanga to Thousand Oaks was only a bit more than half an hour — when Rudy was sick, she told Donna, Sheeba made the drive almost every week.

"We weren't very close, but I felt an obligation," she said. "When your loved ones begin to die, you'll know what I mean." Donna found it interesting that Aunt Sheeba acknowledged that Rudy wasn't necessarily a "loved one" to Donna. It was a peculiar distinction.

"So you got closer as you got older?" Donna asked, trying to put together the story.

"Oh goodness, no," Aunt Sheeba said. "Going to visit her was a chore. Not a terrible chore, I didn't resent it by any means. But I never fully understood Rudy, and then I understood her even less when she was sick. You see?"

Strangely, Donna did see. Sickness and death could bring families closer together — but in the instances of both her father and her Grandmother Rudy, the deaths left feelings of emptiness and confusion. As Donna grew older, she had begun to resent family members who didn't keep in touch. To her, family was supposed to always be there. So when certain family members didn't care about that loyalty, it left a sour taste in Donna's mouth.

"It seems like she traveled a lot," Donna said. "I found knickknacks from places all over the world."

"Oh, yes," Aunt Sheeba went on. "She loved to see the world, and always did bring back something for me. Come to think of it, I think gifts were her love language — but they aren't mine, so I never knew what to do with all that crap." It was interesting to Donna that Rudy was being painted as the distant one when her Aunt Sheeba was the one who was coming across as crabby, like a real pain. Her tone was almost grating, but it was clear she loved to gossip. In between thoughts, Donna could hear her excitedly crunching on ice. "She was very reclusive. But she fell in love, as I'm sure you know, soon before she died. Well, she would never admit it to anyone, but we could all plainly see she was in love."

"Who is 'we all'?" Donna wanted to know.

"Well, me, my husband, and our daughters," Aunt Sheeba said, then took another big crunch.

"Did she meet someone at the hospital?"

"Oh yes." Aunt Sheeba put it as though she were describing a scandal. "One of her caretakers."

"That's odd," Donna said. "What happened to him?"

"I'm not sure," Aunt Sheeba said, "Your grandmother was very secretive about him. I met him a handful of times, but from what I gather they spent a lot of time together."

"He loved her, too . . . ?" Donna trailed off. It was depressing. She had never heard of this man, and everyone made her grandmother out to be such a recluse. Maybe there was one person in the world who understood her.

"I don't know about that," Aunt Sheeba said. She coughed. "He loved her, but to be honest I think she was a bit delusional about the whole thing. I don't mean that to sound glib — I know she had a brain tumor — but I think she was especially delusional about Davey."

"Davey was his name?"

"David. But Davey was all she could talk about. Davey this, Davey that. It was exhausting."

Donna paused. She was trying to understand what was weird.

"He was much younger than her."

"Oh."

"*Much* younger." There was another long pause. "Do you see what I'm getting at?"

Donna didn't. "Young women marry older men all the time. I don't know that it's that weird besides, you know, flipping the stereotype."

"I don't mean that, Donna. I'm talking about money."

Alarm bells went off in Donna's head. No wonder she hadn't heard about Davey. The family probably wanted to keep the information contained so he wouldn't get any of her grandmother's money.

"We had to keep a close eye that he wasn't in the will," her aunt went on. "People abuse the elderly like that, you know. They seek them out when they're not in their right state of mind and take advantage."

The thought of someone taking advantage of her sick grandmother made Donna uncomfortable.

"But do you think it was real?" Donna wanted to know. "The love?"

"Oh come on, Donna," her aunt said. "Who gives a shit?"

"I just want to make sure she wasn't alone," Donna said. "That's sort of why I'm doing this project. I just wanted to see what she was up to."

"No one knows what she was up to," her aunt said. "She was chronically *vague*."

"Okay." Donna sighed deeply and thanked her aunt for her time.

"How is it in the house?" she asked.

"It's comfortable," Donna said.

"Just don't be too much like her, Donna," her aunt warned. "She was a good girl, a good sister, a good contributor to society. But she didn't let people in. She moved into that house and shut everyone out. I don't want you to be like that." She crunched a couple of nuggets of ice then said, "She never was married, you know, which is unusual for our generation." This made Donna take a deep pause. She thought of her absent father, then of her father's absent father. She was suddenly terrified of being in a family tree with generations of absent parents. If she ever did have children, she needed to ensure this didn't happen.

"I won't be like that," Donna promised. "I'm fine."

"You gonna come visit me?" Aunt Sheeba asked. "I'm healthy but won't be around long, you know." Donna rolled her eyes. Talking to Sheeba was exhausting.

"Absolutely," she forced out. But she did want to know one more thing. "Aunt Sheeba," she asked, "do you think there is any way I could get in touch with Davey?"

Her aunt sighed. "I'm glad you want to know so much about your family," she said. "Let me call the hospital. I'll see what I can find out."

* * *

It was days before Donna heard from her aunt again. In the meantime, she didn't see Joshua, not even once. They avoided each other in tandem. She became attuned to his every movement and could hear the rhythm of his breath when he was about to get up and enter the room. She knew when he went to the bathroom. She knew when he was about to end a phone call. She even knew when he was about to put his pencil down, put his laptop away, lie down, stand up. They were closer than ever in proximity, further than ever in intimacy. Neither party left the house unless they absolutely had to. They were in a silent war over it.

One day at the salon, a client named Marie was getting a blowout, and Donna explained the escalating living situation to her and Lydia. Lydia shut off the blow dryer and recommended Donna call a lawyer. Marie was an elderly regular who came to the salon more for social interaction than for her hair. She nodded in agreement.

"He's playing you like a harp," Marie said. "Squatters are scary motherfuckers, pardon my mouth. Didn't you read that story in *New York Mag*?"

"I read it," Lydia said, sticking a bobby pin in her mouth.

"What happened?" Donna asked. She had only heard about squatters in scary news stories and urban legends — it had never occurred to her one could be in her midst.

Marie turned her wheely chair to face Donna square on. "Some girl, some nice girl — like you — put up a room on Craigslist and the next thing you know, some godsend moves in to help pay the bills and fill the room." She leaned back, exasperated. "Of course, it was too good to be true."

"What do you mean?" Donna asked.

"Oh, all kinds of nonsense. He was a con who swindled her out of rent, became violent, ruined her life. And you know what's more?" she said as Lydia spun her back to face the mirror. "The courts didn't look after her at all. It was a domestic dispute — he had lived there so long he had the rights of an owner."

"Mhm," Lydia went on. "And the cat shit."

"What cat shit?" Donna asked, panicked.

"He was clogging up the toilet with cat shit, hoarding bullets in the house, it was all very dangerous," Marie said.

"Was she okay?' Donna gulped.

"Yes," Marie said. "But it was a close one." Lydia stuck one more pin into Marie's hair and began to spray. "It looks beautiful, Lydia, as always." After her smock was removed, she got up and pulled a generous cash tip out of her purse. Donna sat on a nearby chair, tensely.

"Thank you," said Lydia. Then she turned to Donna. "You should call the cops."

"And say what?" Donna wanted to know. "What law has he broken?"

"He's holding himself hostage in your house," Lydia said. "Isn't that enough?"

"I was stupid," Donna admitted. "I didn't have him sign a lease or anything." She gulped. "I just . . . liked him."

"Are you kidding me?" Marie asked and pursed her lips. "My god." Lydia didn't look pleased, either. Donna felt like the two women were facing her in battle. She was about to make some excuse to walk away — maybe go to the bathroom, handle some restock — but then Marie pulled out a checkbook. "Listen to me," she said. "This isn't much, but you need to call a lawyer. I know many do consultations for a hundred an hour." She handed Donna a check. "Here's your first hour. Don't spend it anywhere else."

"Thank you," Donna said. Lydia glared at her and sighed.

When the door closed and the bell made its little tinkle sound, Lydia continued the interrogation. "Why weren't you more careful? You can't trust everybody you meet."

"Don't say that," Donna said. "I was new here — eager to make friends."

"You had me right away," Lydia said.

"I know I had you, but you have your own life. I was — I don't know — it can be scary living by yourself. I had never done it before."

"Well, it's scarier now," Lydia concluded. "I can assure you that."

There was a long pause. Lydia began to sweep the floor. "I got it," Donna intervened, and took the broom.

"What's next?" Lydia asked.

"You have a cut and color in thirty minutes," Donna sniffled.

"No, Donna, I mean what's next with the lawyer? You're gonna use that money, right?"

"Yes," Donna said. "I will today."

"I'm gonna hold you accountable," said Lydia, and went out back for a smoke.

* * *

Donna called a few lawyers during her lunch break, and most of them were insensitive to her circumstances. It was a difficult situation to explain — Donna had trouble skirting around the innate problem, which is that she had walked confidently and blindly into a trap.

After toggling with a series of smug men, she finally reached an LA-based domestic dispute lawyer named Roberta, who seemed to be an assassin at her job and who Donna jived with a lot. Roberta was a California native who specialized in domestic abuse but had handled a squatter case before. "But it doesn't just end there," she said. "In the state of California, if you've been living in a home for six months, then it becomes a domestic case."

"Great," Donna said, dryly. "So how do we get started?"

"Domestic cases are the hardest in court," Roberta said. "It's hard to verify accusations. A lot of it is 'he said, she said.' You'll want to be prepared before we begin, or else we're screwed." And the other thing was, Roberta was expensive. "I know it costs a lot of money," Roberta said. "Save everything you can. Start to collect everything. Write everything down. Record anything that seems funky. When you do call me back — and I'm sure you will — we can maximize your time."

Donna thanked her even though she was deeply resentful that Joshua had become someone who was in her domestic periphery.

"One more piece of advice?" Roberta added. "You need to be home whenever you can. Like in a marriage, if he can prove that you left, the house is his. And what's worse — he can lock it up."

"No nights out," Donna repeated. Got it.

It was hard not leaving, but Donna kept her word. She wanted to stay at Cole's in his peaceful studio apartment, and for the first time, she missed living in a trash apartment. She felt like the space was more hers crammed into a home with multiple roommates than in her big, lonely grandmother's house with Joshua. She felt she was living in Joshua's toxic nightmare shadow. Every day was another disaster. To make matters worse, Joshua was no longer showering. She was convinced it was because he was trying to amplify his smell. He wanted the place to reek.

In her love life, Cole was visibly hurt by Donna's distance. For him, it was a lose-lose — she was adamant about not staying at his apartment, but also resistant to inviting him to her house too much. Without the full context, Donna worried, Cole would suspect she was losing interest and trying to edge him out. So after talking to Roberta, Donna gained new confidence in how to handle the house. It would be her house and Joshua could deal with that however sourly he wanted. She began watching television loudly in the common area. She spoke loudly to Cole, cooked elaborate dinners, and soaked up every second in the shared space that she could. Even though Joshua never came out of his room, she wanted him to know he was not welcome. She wanted him to know the space was hers.

Everything seemed to be going swimmingly until one day Joshua left a formal, typewritten note in a business envelope under Donna's door. The note was dated and signed by Joshua, had a place for Donna to sign as well, and said that if the following occurrences were not remedied, he would be forced to call the police. The occurrences included a list of domestic complaints, ending lastly with urinating in plastic bottles.

Donna's pee in the water bottles, Joshua emphasized, rendered the home particularly uninhabitable. "You frequently leave your door unlocked and even open," Joshua went on, "and so the matter contaminates my space."

Donna was appalled. The few times she had peed in the bottle were to avoid Joshua, and she threw them away the morning after. The note made Donna certain that Joshua was rummaging through her room on a daily basis, or at the very least rummaging through the trash outside. She felt exposed, like he was looking for any small thing in the world to sue her. He wanted her out of the bungalow or worse, dead, but she couldn't think about the second one. She felt like she had a stalker, and the stalker was considered to be her domestic partner.

CHAPTER FOURTEEN: THE BIRTHDAY PARTY

She obviously did not sign the document and Joshua did not seem to care. The fact that he didn't care made the event even more stressful. It showed that he was watching her, that he wanted her to know that he had an eye on her. The letter had been a warning. Donna whispered about it to Cole in her bedroom. She was still avoiding going to Cole's house with the fear that Joshua would replace all the locks and she would be stuck out of the house. Cole whispered back about Joshua, but he felt a strain being in her home and didn't stay overnight often, either. The house was plagued with a negative feeling, he said, and it wasn't anything he had experienced in a long time. "It reminds me of my exes," he said brashly one day. "And it's not even your fault, but I think you could do more to fix it."

"Fix it?" Donna barked. "What am I supposed to do?"

"Donna," Cole said, calmly. "I'm just trying to tell you how I feel."

Donna had never been adequate at handling men's feelings. They perplexed her. Why did men have to feel things? She wanted to be the only person in the world who was allowed to feel things.

One sunny and eerily California-ish day, Joshua entered the living area breezily like nothing was wrong.

"Morning," he said. He was clean. His hair was washed and his clothes unwrinkled. He must have taken a long shower to prepare for this strange morning chat.

"Hi," Donna said coldly. Her ribs were pulsing. She was afraid of what Joshua had to say.

"Listen," he said. "It's my birthday on Friday."

Donna shrugged. She didn't know what he expected from her.

"I don't need anything from you," Joshua said, "but I'd love to have a party here if you are okay with it. You are my roommate, so I wanted to run it by you."

"Why do you suddenly care what I think?" Donna hissed brashly. "You never cared before." She was trying not to cry, but the very presence of Joshua made her eyes sting.

"I like you, Donna," he said. "I really do."

"You move into my house," she grunted, "refuse to pay me my rent, insult my boyfriend, threaten me, and then want to throw some kind of mega bash here for your birthday?"

"It's not a mega bash," he promised. "It will be a few people. A dinner party. It will be simple," he said, alluding to Ina Garten. "How easy is that?"

Donna's nerves spiked. She hated that she wanted to laugh at his Ina Garten joke. How dare he enter the room confidently and act like an exemplary roommate? She wanted to kill him.

"What do you say?"

"Absolutely not."

"Why not?"

"Because I don't want to throw you a party," she said. Her insult cut through the room like a shard of broken window.

"I'm turning forty," said Joshua. "It's big for me."

Donna looked into Joshua's eyes and squinted. He squinted too. He was mirroring her expression. He looked older than forty, but Donna wondered if it was because she was now skeptical of his every move. Did his mother even die this year? Did he even have friends to invite to a party? Everything felt like a test.

"Who is going to come?" she asked.

"My brother and sister," he said. "A couple friends from work."

"I thought you worked remote."

"We still have a team," Joshua said. "And we could invite Cole."

"Who else."

"What do you mean who else?"

"I mean who else? You're really asking me permission to have like five people over for a quiet birthday dinner?"

"Well, yes," he said. Donna squinted harder at him. He squinted back.

"I'm not getting you a present," she said.

"But I can have the party?" he asked.

Donna considered it. She certainly did not want to concede to anything he wanted — nor did she want to celebrate the day of his birth — but she wondered if the party could be a window for her to meet other people in Joshua's life and learn more about him. She had a hard time believing there were people who loved him and wanted to celebrate him. Who were these people? And why were they so stupid?

"The year has been hard," Joshua continued. "I'm not myself. You met me at a weird time." And then, worst of all, "I miss you."

Donna winced at his affection but did begrudgingly agree to let him have the party. Against her better judgment, she was unendingly curious to meet his friends and family. She needed to see him in a different context of people. She had to know if he was likable, upstanding, a hardworking employee with funny jokes and taste and candor. She wanted to see him again as she had seen him the first time they met. She needed that, and she needed Cole to see that, for the sake of her honest and perceived sanity.

"Can I invite a friend of my own?" she asked.

"Besides Cole?" Joshua wanted to know.

"Her name is Lydia," Donna replied. "She works with me at the salon." If Lydia wanted to hold Donna accountable to act against Joshua, it would be beneficial for the two to meet. Plus, Donna was dying to know what Lydia would think of him, in the flesh.

"That's fine," Joshua said briskly. "I look forward to meeting her."

Over a bottle of wine later that night, Donna told Cole about the party. "What are we supposed to wear?" she asked.

"It's your house," he said. "Who cares what you wear? I can't even believe you said yes to him."

"I think he wants to put on a show for us," Donna said. "And I want to find out what it is."

"I told you a long time ago I thought he needed to leave," Cole said. "With him still here I'm just like . . . what's the point? Do you put up with all this because you're bored or like the drama?"

"You didn't know him before his mom died," Donna said. "It was different. He and I were a natural match."

"I'll come," he said, sighing. "But I need to be honest that this isn't . . . as much fun lately, Donna."

"I'm fun," she insisted. But she was frazzled — she knew she wasn't giving Cole her all.

"Okay," Cole said, packing up his bag. "I'll be there, but I have a work event first. I'll come when I can."

* * *

Lydia was also reluctant about her RSVP.

"Aren't you at least curious?" Donna asked.

"You know I am," Lydia said, "but you're making trouble."

"Please," Donna begged. She wanted her friend's validation. Lydia begrudgingly agreed, under the condition that she could leave whenever she wanted with no hard feelings. She admitted being afraid about coming over. "What if he flips his shit?" she laughed maniacally. "And like breaks all your furniture or, like, kills everyone?"

She didn't want to admit it, but ever since Joshua had left Donna the threatening note, she had fears, too. Like he wanted to observe everyone quietly, take notes and blackmail them later. She hoped, desperately, he was just a lonely man who was turning forty and needed people to ring in the year with him.

Aunt Sheeba didn't call again but sent an email.

Dear Donna,

I wasn't able to get a hold of Davey. I talked to multiple people at the hospital. At first, I thought they were just trying to protect his information. But after I told them how close he was to your grandmother, I think they don't know where he is, either. He didn't work there long after she died. And by the sounds of it, I think he moved away.

All my love,
Sheeba

P.S. I'm sorry if I was harsh with you. She really was a lovely woman — in the end I am just bitter, I think, that I wasn't closer with my sister.

Best of luck with your project. Come to Thousand Oaks for a visit.

Donna was sad she wouldn't be able to reach Davey, but she felt like it wasn't over. She created a page for him in her grandmother's binder and left it blank. Their love story didn't feel complete.

* * *

On Friday, she headed out the salon door right at five so she could get home and mentally prepare herself for the party.

Joshua's brother was the first to arrive. When the doorbell rang, Joshua was out getting ice. It was a potluck party, but he made a few dishes while Donna was away. It was truly

Ina Garten-inspired. Joshua had hung a delicate string of fairy lights over the kitchen island. The food table featured easy cocktails and easy hors d'oeuvres and everything — from the spicy lemon and arugula salad to the honey-baked brie to the watermelon bruschetta — looked delicious.

Joshua's brother, Gabriel, did not look or act much like Joshua at all. He was athletic, trim, tall and dressed in a sleek black North Face zip-up. His pants and shoes were casual but pressed, like those of a typical fit man who lived in LA. His face did carry the same pleasant expression that Joshua's did, when he wasn't looking so jaded. His eyebrows were black and so was his hair, except for a few nice gray patches. For some reason, Donna expected he would be bald, too. But he had nice hair and a nice face. He seemed friendly and put together.

She invited him in, and there was a tense moment when she wondered what all he knew about her. She wondered if she could trust him, or if he was there to scam her as well. But he behaved politely. He removed his shoes when he entered, asked if he should hang up his jacket. He asked Donna questions about her grandmother and her boyfriend and her job. It was small talk but unencumbered by too much of an obligatory feeling. It felt easy.

During their entire encounter, Donna felt hyper-aware of him. She tried to pull apart his every move based on how like or unlike Joshua he was. She assumed he was single, based on the way he acted. Coupled men always had a certain anxiety about them, being alone with a woman. But Gabriel seemed completely at ease with Donna. She wondered if he thought she was pretty, though she wasn't sure why.

Donna offered to make him a drink, but he was a step ahead of her. He asked what kind of liquor she liked, and he went to make them both a bourbon on ice. He was comfortable in the kitchen, which she attributed to being LA-style classy, and he also seemed wealthy, based on his comfortable, entitled behavior. It was his generosity, maybe, the same kind of generosity Joshua used to possess.

Next, Lydia arrived. Donna sighed in gratitude. She didn't want to be trapped with Gabriel and Joshua before any of her people showed up. She wasn't sure how Lydia would act but was relieved to catch her charismatic and upbeat. Lydia was as graceful as Gabriel. She had changed out of her day clothes, too, and wore a flowy red maxi dress and a pair of stilettos. She trod gracefully, barely making a sound. Donna had noticed that California people didn't struggle nearly as much in social situations as the Midwesterners and Lydia and Gabriel immediately exchanged some flirtation, which was fine, so long as Lydia kept her eye on the mission.

Lydia was also very pleased to see the house. She had heard so much about it, she kept saying, and giving Donna a subtle wink.

"Are you going to give me a tour?" she asked, and Donna obliged.

She took them into the bathroom and her bedroom. They ooh'd and ahh'd over the turquoise accents, the finely done kitchen tiles, the structure of the rooms as a whole. Even at night, light seemed to pour in, or at least look like it would pour in, and that made it even more inviting.

They loved the bathtub and the Jack and Jill sink, two touches Donna was proud to show off. It gave her a boost in confidence. "It's like you and Joshua are married," Gabriel joked, "with those sinks."

Donna looked to Lydia and rolled her eyes. She and Joshua did seem married, in more ways than one unfortunately. They were like a tense couple going through a separation. She tried not to let this sarcasm carry in her voice when she made her next comment. "Joshua locks his room, so we won't be able to get in there."

"Does he?" Gabriel asked, his hand on the doorknob. "I don't see a lock."

"Oh yeah," she said. "I'm barely allowed in there. I hardly know what it looks like."

Gabriel and Lydia gave Donna a puzzled look. Donna's eyes went to the knob. There was no lock. Joshua had placed a brand-new, crystal knob on the door. A homey, wealthy-looking knob that obviously had no lock attached to it.

"Looks like he got a new knob," Donna said. "I don't know when that happened." She looked at Lydia in a panic, but Lydia was following Gabriel into Joshua's room.

When they walked in, Donna gasped. The room was pristine. Joshua had placed a gorgeous mahogany headboard behind a tall, queen bed. From the ceiling hung a pendant light with a dark geometric frame. There was a dark gray duvet and fluffy pillows on the bed. In the center, an emerald green throw pillow. Below the bed, there were storage drawers where she assumed Joshua had moved his clothes. The walk-in closet door was open. Inside, Joshua had placed a work desk and a nice, dim lamp, a tiny office sectioned off within the room. Then, there was a big bold dresser with a brightly lit eucalyptus candle. On the dresser, there were a few special-looking collector coins and a nice watch. Above it, a big, bold, rectangular mirror.

But the star of the room was the twenty-foot python, which was coiled perfectly around an exquisite tree branch in a very well-kept snake cage. It was a glorious terrarium — clean and well-ventilated. The snake looked calm and happy, as far as snakes go. Beneath it, there was a small bowl where mice must have gone in to feed it. He was well-watered and spoiled with plants and oxygen and relaxed lighting. The tan room with emerald accents evoked a rainforest. An airy, serene rainforest. What disturbed Donna especially was how clean the air felt. It was as clear as being outdoors, even with the window shut.

"This is amazing," Lydia said, and looked to Donna for confirmation. "I don't know what I expected," she said. "But I did not expect this."

"I knew my Joshua was stylin', but . . ." Gabriel added. "This is something else."

Donna's feet melted into the carpet. She was shocked. The room's lighting was sophisticated. It smelled nice. Her room hadn't been this clean in ages, if ever. There was a brand-new green-and-black Turkish rug covering the floor. All of it looked expensive, cozy and miraculous. Her stomach filled with jealous bile. She needed Joshua to get the fuck out.

She thought of her own room and how she proudly showed it off. Her stupid rug. Her stupid bed. Her stupid quilt. They were things she had placed there because they made her happy and they were affordable. She hated herself and her style and her taste. She hated everything about herself. She was on fire with fury.

* * *

By the time Joshua arrived, his sister and two of his friends had shown up. Everyone made the party so far except Cole. Joshua was cool and understated. He didn't make a big scene about his bedroom or about turning forty. While everyone coated him with compliments, he stood still and appreciative and rosy.

Donna tried to make eye contact with him several times. She wanted him to lock his gaze with hers so she could tell him "I know what you're up to and I don't like it," but every time he did meet her eyes, he smiled coyly. It was a game of who could stay on the rocker long enough before completely flipping out.

Joshua's sister, Iona, was less rich-looking than Gabriel. Still, she was cute. She had a freckled face and wore a subdued baby blue blouse. Under that, a poorly fit but still acceptable black pencil skirt and blue sandals. It appeared as though she had just gotten out of an office job. She wasn't wearing makeup and had the same healthy complexion Joshua and Gabriel shared. It was the only thing Donna could find in common between the three of them. Seeing her, Donna wondered what their mother had looked like. She had probably been fresh-faced, too.

During appetizers, everyone split off into their own conversations. Gabriel and Lydia flirted in the corner — they were clearly and elegantly matched. Joshua amused his friends at the kitchen island. That left Donna with Iona.

Iona was talkative, more so than Donna. She was also eerily bubbly for a woman whose mother had recently died. Donna wanted to ask about it, but it never felt like the right time.

"So sick to see his new digs," she said, munching on a bite of crostini.

"Had you been to his other places?" Donna asked. She tried to ask pointed questions in a way that didn't pry or seem obvious she was completely uneasy.

"Oh, yeah," Iona said. "I've seen them all. Lovers have come and gone, cities came in and out of the picture, jobs, you know how it is. This place is great! Nothing I can dig him on."

"Iona, stop harassing my roommate," Joshua said playfully. "What did she say to you?"

"She said she doesn't have much to make you feel bad about right now," Donna said. "Which I find hard to believe." Everyone in the room laughed. It seemed fun and playful, so Donna pushed a little harder. "You should have seen his room before today," Donna said. "It was pretty gross."

The laughter subsided, but not enough to render the comment completely cold.

"She's not wrong," Joshua agreed. "I did as much as I can to prove myself as a worthy forty-year-old."

"Cheers to that," said Gabriel, and everybody drank.

"Donna, I thought Cole was coming by," Joshua said.

"He is," Donna responded defensively. "I don't know where he is."

"Make him get here, Donna!" said Lydia. "I want to be sure I see him."

"Well, you aren't going anywhere soon, right?" Joshua asked. "You'll have plenty of time."

Still, Donna was worried. She went to the front of the house and stared helplessly at the street. She prayed Cole's headlights would show up, making their casual way into the front yard. Cole was the only thing that would make her feel less uncomfortable. She stood there a long while. More food came out of the oven and more cocktails were poured. Lydia returned to Donna periodically to make sure she was okay. Everything was going fine, she supposed, but for some reason she was worried about Cole. She tried to call him several times. Nothing. It just rang and rang and hit voicemail. Donna hated leaving voicemails but left one for Cole anyway. It was her gesture of true love. "Where are you?" she whispered. "Save me."

When everyone was nice and toasty, Gabriel asked Joshua if they could bring the snake out.

"No," Donna said insistently. "Absolutely not."

"Oh, come on, Donna," said Gabriel. "It's Joshua's birthday."

Then the friends were chanting, "Donna! Donna! Donna!" and Joshua looked deeply into Donna's eyes and said, "Please? Just this once?"

* * *

It took a while to get the snake out of a cage. Joshua had to use a stepladder. The snake's eye seemed to look at no one and everyone at once. Its eyes held a kind of numb contact that seemed distant and intimate with everyone.

Joshua placed its heavy body on the ground, and it relaxed into a comfortable squiggle. At first, it was like looking at an animal in the zoo — it was careful, cautious, and seemed safe. Then, when the group became more confident, so did the snake.

Its movements became faster and more certain. At some points, it darted to a member of the circle and everyone would scream. Then, it would pull back. It took a special liking to Donna, who was the least interested in it. Lydia adored the snake and said she used to have one just as big. Donna highly doubted that, yet she was intrigued by the lack of fear Lydia possessed.

"I've never been into snakes," Gabriel explained. "But this one is pretty damn cool." Gabriel asked if he could feed the snake some of the dinner meat the group ate.

"He won't eat it," Joshua said. "He likes his food live, so he can feel like he's hunting."

"Well do you have any live food?" Lydia wanted to know. "I want to see him eat."

"I do, in fact," said Joshua. He walked into the closet and opened a large white bin. Inside the bin, in a disgusting moving pile, were dozens of wriggling mice. As he closed the lid, Donna caught a whiff of the mice's smell. She realized what she had been smelling all this time was not the snake, but mice all on top of one another defecating and doing their best to survive.

"Can I feed it?" asked Gabriel.

"Do you want to do it the easy way or the fun way?" Josh asked.

"'The fun way' sounds like it's gonna scare me shitless," Iona said.

Donna was in a corner clutching the walls. She remembered her encounter on the floor with this creature. The way it measured her.

"Do you mind being a little scared?" Joshua asked, and the group agreed no. They liked it.

Joshua lifted the mouse above his head and caught the snake's eye with it, which dilated and pulsed with pleasure. It was hungry. It was like seeing a perfectly cooked filet for the first time, but a filet you would have to work for. Joshua slowly lowered the mouse onto the ground and held it for a moment. The mouse's tiny hands and feet were moving crazily; it wanted to run.

Joshua let it run in place for a moment before he released it. Once he pulled up his hand, the mouse began to sprint towards the walls, desperately searching for an exit. The snake moved its body in a wave and collected itself in the corner of the group, in a small coil. He crept up on the mouse, playing with it. The mouse darted to another wall, still looking for a place to exit. The snake's eyes narrowed. He was sizing up his lunch which in size comparison was merely a crouton. A quick, anxious, panicked crouton.

When the mouse ran to another side, the snake lengthened and moved in a wave again. The group screamed and jumped to the side. Joshua warned everyone to not get too excited, that they could scare the snake with too much energy.

Finally, the snake lunged at the mouse and dug its teeth into the rodent's tiny neck. Rather than just chomping down on it and ending its life, though, it began to wrap and wrap its body around the mouse's body. The mouse was being killed slowly, painfully, losing its last breath. The group watched the life fade from the mouse's eyes.

The entire charade felt like an eternity. Then, everybody clapped.

The snake sat in unimpressed glory, seeming like it just wanted more to eat. Its flexible body was astounding; how was it so sturdy and so loose at the same time? When Donna looked at it, she imagined all the clothing that could be made from its skin. With twenty feet in length, it could probably make at least ten pairs of shoes. Or one jacket. But even though the color was mesmerizing, she found it hideous. She would never purchase anything like it.

Joshua's friends were stranger than his siblings. They all seemed like misfits, with something wrong with each of them. They held their own with reserved auras of awkwardness: yellow teeth, greasy hair, unbuttoned sleeves. They weren't the sort of guys she would get to know if she wasn't forced to. Next to them, Joshua seemed especially charming.

To make everything worse, the strange friends were fawning over the snake. It was apparent they were video game fantasy nerds, people who always pretended they had snakes and dragons but never actually had them. Donna pictured they were the sort of boys who kept rattlesnake rattles on their desks or wore snake tooth necklaces with faux leather straps.

It was also obvious that each of these strange men wanted to be close to Donna. They kept emphasizing how wonderful it was to meet her, how they had heard so much about her. Donna didn't know how well they knew Joshua, though. In his elusive online work, did he have a lot of networking opportunities? Why hadn't she heard of these people before today?

As she speculated, Cole finally arrived. He walked in without knocking, which gave Donna a feeling of comfort and stability. "You're here!" she shouted, and ran into his skinny arms.

"I'm so sorry," Cole said. "My coworkers went out for a happy hour and it was one round after another." His breath smelt a bit toasty. She hoped he had been okay driving.

"Why didn't you respond to my calls?" she asked quietly.

"My phone died," he said, then noticed Donna looked deflated. "How is everything going?" he whispered.

"Surprisingly well," Donna said, "for everyone except me."

"Cole!" said Joshua, closing in for an embrace. "You had a pre-party of your own?"

"Sure," Cole said, looking surprised at Joshua's friendliness. "Sorry I'm late."

"I'm sure Donna will be much more at ease now that you're here," Joshua said, which Donna took as an insult.

"We're having a fine time," she said spitefully. "I'll fix you a plate. You had enough to drink?"

Aware that he had disappointed Donna, she presumed, he said he would take a glass of water for now. The party carried on in a dull roar until almost 2 a.m. When the guests left, Joshua thanked Donna profusely for allowing him to throw the party.

"It was the best night since . . . I can even remember," he said. And he even insisted Cole stay the night — they could all sleep in and have brunch in the morning. On the surface, it had been fun.

CHAPTER FIFTEEN: OPEN CAGE

They did not have brunch. The day after the birthday party, Joshua had a tantrum. There was a sink full of dishes and small pieces of wrapping paper all over the floor. The bathroom looked used up by all the guests and there was no toilet paper left on the roll. There were plastic cups all over the place — all remnants of others in their usually sacred apartment. Lydia had left her high heels after kicking them off and driving home barefoot. One of the workers had left a tote bag filled with dirty Tupperware. Another left a mound of undesirable candy. Donna assumed the person who left the candy was trying to be polite. The refrigerator was filled with dips and leftover meats and cheeses. The chips were left open on the counter, bound to go stale.

Joshua had a tantrum because of how deeply the status of the house overwhelmed him. He saw the consequences of the bash he threw and that it involved cleaning and restoration. Both of which, Donna presumed, he was uncomfortable with.

"Aren't you going to help me?" he asked in the morning as Donna sat on the sofa, making a to-do list for her day. Cole was still asleep in bed — he and Joshua were both off on Saturdays.

"I will help you," she said calmly. "But I can't do it now. I am leaving soon."

"It's trashed, Donna," he said. He sounded panicked.

"It wasn't my party," she said, and stood to walk to the bathroom. Joshua wedged his body in front of hers, blocking her from the door. "What do you want?" she asked.

"You were right," Joshua said, fear in his eyes. "I shouldn't have thrown a party."

"I thought you had fun," she said, her tone still hostile.

"But was it worth it?" he asked, rhetorically. "It was too much pressure. I put too much pressure on myself."

"You can say that again."

"What's that supposed to mean?"

"What the hell is going on with your room?" Donna asked. This time, her voice came out more venomous than she intended. She paused for a moment and considered pulling back in. There was something about Joshua's demeanor that put her on edge, and she didn't want to push him too far so early in the morning.

"I thought you'd be pleased," he said. "I cleaned it up."

"If you don't care about material stuff, then why would you buy all that stuff?" she asked.

"To impress," he said. His eyes narrowed and seemed to look past her for a moment. Then, he cocked his head. "Are you jealous?" he asked.

"Absolutely," she said. "Where did you get all that money?"

"What do you mean?" he asked.

"If you struggle so much to pay rent, then how can you afford that aquarium? That headboard, those lights?"

"It's a terrarium," Joshua said. He laughed. He didn't seem nervous anymore.

"What's funny?" Donna pressed.

"I don't struggle to pay rent, Donna," he stated. "I just don't like doing it."

Donna's cheeks faded to white.

"I need you to pick this place up," she commanded. "Before I get home."

"No," he said.

"What?"

"No."

"Why not?"

"Because I don't want to."

"You're a child," Donna said.

She pivoted on her heels and began to walk away. But as she did, Joshua let out a big scream. He jumped up and down and shrieked, his face turning red, and real tears began to stream down his face. He was sweaty in an instant and looked so hot that he could burn. He screamed and stomped his feet into the hardwood floor. He batted at the wall with his hand and continued to scream. "I'm a child!" he screamed. "Put me in time out then!"

"Joshua—" she started.

"Put me in time out!" he went on. His voice was shrill.

Donna had never seen an adult behave this way. The authenticity of his tears terrified her. It was the best performance she had ever seen.

"Joshua," she started. "I need you to stop right now."

"No," he cried. "No, Mommy, no."

This made Donna so angry she could hardly breathe. She huffed and got close to his face. "Joshua Flowers," she growled. "I need you to fucking stop it or I'm calling the police."

"No!" he kicked. The tears streamed harder. "No, no, no!"

Enraged, Donna smacked Joshua in the face as hard as she could. It was a clumsy punch. Her knuckles landed somewhere between his brow bone and his forehead, the force making a slight knocking sound.

For a second, Joshua looked as though he was in pain. But his face twisted up and seemed graceful for a moment — pleasant, even — but then contorted into a darkened grin. At first, Donna wanted to laugh. She couldn't believe the range of expression he went through before her eyes. But then she remembered her anger and her fear. She felt immediate regret. Would he punch her back? Grab her by the hair and strangle her? But it was worse. He calmly wiped his tears and smiled. His tight smile was the smile of pure evil, and he began to giggle, and giggle, and giggle like a child. Like a psychopathic child. Like a child on the late-night specials that were like, "I have known my child was possessed since he was three years old."

Joshua Flowers may as well have been possessed as a child. And even though his forehead would soon darken into a purple bruise, Donna knew he was winning. And the thought of him winning terrified her.

CHAPTER SIXTEEN: THE WRITHING WEST

After the bizarre tantrum, Donna found it necessary for Cole to spend the night at her place as much as possible. She basically cornered him into it. Every day when she got off work, she called and demanded to know his whereabouts. If he was at his place doing his own thing, she became angry. If Cole wasn't there, Donna was certain Cole didn't have any concern about her well-being. Couldn't he see she was living with someone who was potentially lethal?

"I think you should move out," he said, which put Donna into even more of a fury.

"Don't you understand? If I move out, I'm giving up this gorgeous house. I'm conceding to the villain."

"But what connection do you have to this house anyway?" he asked.

"Well, everything, if I could just get him the fuck out!" Donna said.

"Then why did you bring him here in the first place? You weren't content here when it was just you."

"But then I met you," Donna said.

"So what — you want me to move in and replace Joshua and make this all disappear? Then what, we're just together forever? Homeowners living on some inheritance in Topanga?"

Cole's words stung Donna. She felt like he was implying she was rich, which was far from the truth. "This house is all I have," she said.

"Yeah," Cole argued, "and do you know how much it's worth?"

"What are you implying?"

"This place sucks, Donna," he said. "It's ruined you. Sell it and you're sitting on 800 grand cash easily. Maybe even 900. Maybe even a million," he paused. "Have you ever even taken the time to look it up?"

Donna was frozen. Selling the house had never crossed her mind. "Cole," she said. "The point of the house isn't *cash*."

"Then what is it?" he demanded. "Because it sounds to me like you hate this place."

Donna was quiet for a second, panicking. It was their first real fight. She had never had a romantic fight, certainly not to this degree. In comparison, their arguments were like siblings bickering. "Can we change the tone?" Donna asked. "You're making me nervous."

"Why?" Cole said.

"Are you going to break up with me?"

Taking in her fear, Cole softened. "No," he said. "No." But after a pause, he went on. "But listen, I wonder if we should take a step back. We met and things happened so fast. I felt like it was easy — there was a natural, effortless connection with you. Now—" he paused. "Now . . . all this drama is making me feel like I'm not getting a proper chance to get to know you. Your life seems very complicated."

"You do know me," Donna said, her voice choked.

"I really don't," Cole contested. "Listen — I know it feels like I do. And I do want to know every part of you. But we're not doing that normal couple thing, you know — the honeymoon thing — and I don't want us to get off on a bad start."

Donna felt paralyzed. It all came crashing into her — his distance, why he was late to the party, why he was barely remorseful when he was out of touch. But in her defense, she added, "I can't be sorry for being a lot. I am who I am."

"I know," Cole understood. "And so am I. But I'm like the bass in the background and you're — the electric solo." Donna put her hands on her hips. He was right. Then, he shifted the subject. "It may be worth it to get an appraisal," he said. "Just to know."

"Then what — I sell the house and I do what?"

"Live alone," he said. "Or live with me." Donna pulled a face, puzzled. "*Eventually*," he added.

"You need to cut me some slack," she said. "You're really my first adult relationship."

"Well, you aren't mine," Cole said cautiously. "I need you to cut me some slack, too."

"No," Donna said.

"Yes," he said gently. "At least for a while. If you don't want to get an appraisal, maybe you should still take a hard look at what this home means to you. Because look at you — you're so afraid of even going in the living room, using your own bathroom. That's not what a home is."

"Okay," she said. "I'll think about it."

By now, the party had been over for almost a week. The place was still a disaster. Even though she had been too proud to pick up the mess herself, she finally reasoned it was time. Cole was right, and she didn't want to dwell in filth.

It was early afternoon, and Donna took a shot of bourbon. She had been doing that a lot lately. She wanted to erase herself for a second every time she drank. The reality that she was way in over her head set in vengefully. The longer she stayed in this place with no clue of how to relish it properly, the more she had to reckon with the fact that she was afraid of being incapable. Even though they agreed to take a step back, Cole agreed to help her clean and as soon as he'd arrived, the two set to work.

Amidst the bustling, there were a few moments of quiet. Donna sat in the darkness of her room for a breather, drinking her vodka and listening to the pitter-patter of Cole picking up trash. He was wearing slippers and his footsteps sounded gentle. The trash going into the receptacle was therapeutic, the sound of restoration.

There was a shift in the house. Donna couldn't put her finger on it, but it was like a shadow of bad energy began to cloud the space. Joshua must have emerged from his cave. She wondered if his room was still pristine, all his new belongings in place.

At first, she heard a small murmuring. Then, Cole's voice raised a little. He said something along the lines of, "I don't mind, it's okay." It was hard to hear. The fan was running and bags were rustling and Donna thought the conversation would end there, with Joshua hopefully descending back into his room.

But then, she heard the fridge door slam open, an echo of bottles clanking. Then, she heard Joshua raise his voice much louder than Cole's.

"Do you live here now?" he demanded. "What right do you have?"

"I'm just helping, man," Cole said.

Donna got up and quickly moved into the common space. Joshua and Cole were standing face to face, Cole with a full trash bag and Joshua empty-handed. On the other side of the room, the giant snake slithered intentionally across the floor. The sight of the snake made Donna's stomach flop.

"Your boyfriend is throwing away my belongings," said Joshua. "Don't I have a right to put my possessions where I feel they belong?" he asked.

"Joshua," Donna said. "It's trash. Trash you've neglected to pick up, for *days*."

"You never know the importance of something that belongs to someone else," Joshua said.

"Give me a break," Donna scoffed.

"If I wanted to move my property, don't you think I would have by now?" Joshua asked. When he used terms like "possessions" and "property," it infuriated her. He could be so technical.

"That food is old," Donna said. "It's stinking up the house."

"So he's just going to throw it away?" Joshua asked. "Without consulting me. One of the owners of this house. He's just going to throw it all away."

"I wish he'd throw you away," Donna slurred. She was a little tipsy at this point. "And you don't own this house — despite what my *lawyer* says."

"Donna," Cole interjected. He was trying to save her from oversharing, but Joshua continued.

"Oh, a lawyer? Donna got a lawyer? Because she wants to throw me away? And her boyfriend knows what's trash and what isn't? Well, do you know what's trash to me?" he gestured to the large television. "This."

"Stop, dude," Cole said. "I'll quit throwing away the food. Or better yet — you can tell me what you need me to toss."

"I don't need anything from you," Joshua said. "How about we throw away this?" Joshua asked. He lifted a framed photograph of Donna's grandmother. "Or these?" he gestured to Donna's photographs on the fridge. "Why don't we throw away your martini glasses? Seems like you're just drinking out of the bottle these days anyway."

"Dude, cut it out."

"Dude. Dude," Joshua said. "Dude, dude, dude — I'm a California boy!" he laughed.

Cole ignored him, beginning to aggressively bag up more food and toss it.

"What did I just say, you fucking moron?" Joshua shouted. "Do not touch my food. Do not touch my food. Do not touch my food, dude." The way he repeated himself was grating. Donna thought if he repeated himself one more time, she would lose her shit.

But then he did repeat himself. When Cole went after an aluminum can to put in the garbage, Joshua said, "Put the bag down, put the bag down, dude, put the bag down."

She shouted, "Shut the fuck up!" and the room turned to ice.

"You need to get this guy out, Donna," Cole said. "Call the police. Now."

"Call the police and what?" Joshua taunted. "Tell them we're arguing?"

"You are harassing her," Cole went on. "Can't you have some respect?"

"No," said Joshua. "Respect is something you have for elders, and I am your elder. I need both of you to sit down."

"Or what?" pressed Cole. "Why do you need us to sit down?"

"Cole, I said sit."

Donna felt suddenly afraid and did as he said. She told Cole to do the same, but he stood tall and unwavering.

Joshua took one of the cans and brought it to the kitchen sink. He grabbed a sharp cutting knife from the knife box and stabbed a hole in the can. Then, he pulled slowly and sternly. The sound of the cutting can screeched, like the sound of a hundred dinner forks dragging on a plate in unison.

When the sound was finally over, he lifted the piece of the can he had cut. It was in the shape of a nightmare, darker than a needle or a knife or even a gun. A common domestic item turned evil. Joshua turned his attention back to Cole.

"Cole," he said. "This is my house."

Cole was quiet.

"And if I ask you not to touch my possessions, I need you to obey me," Joshua said. He was still wielding the aluminum weapon. He moved it closer and closer to Cole's face. "If you don't do what I ask, we are going to have problems," he said. "I didn't want a second roommate. Two is company. Three is a crowd."

"You're the third—" Cole interjected.

"Shhh," Joshua shushed. It was maternal-sounding, nurturing. "I'm not done."

He turned to Donna and smiled. "I think it's time we set up a few rules regarding our boyfriends, Donna. What do you think?"

Hoping to end the situation sooner, Donna agreed. "Yes," she said. "Like what?"

"He can stay here two times a week," Joshua said. "And I don't want to speak to him, and I don't want to hear him, and I don't want him touching anything of mine." He looked back to Cole. "Are we clear? Dude?"

Donna wanted to scream in refusal, but her fear made her nod silently.

"Okay," said Joshua. He began to pull the weapon away from Cole's face.

"No," Cole said, shaking his head. "Absolutely not."

"No?" asked Joshua.

"No. Hard no."

And then, Joshua moved the weapon toward Cole's face as if to slice it. But as Cole pulled his head back in retaliation, Joshua used the can to cut a long, thin sliver of skin out of Cole's arm.

"No?" he asked.

Cole staggered back. "You've lost your mind."

"Answer the question," Joshua said. "Respect, remember?"

"Okay," said Cole. "Okay." He exhaled in compliance, holding up his hands. "Twice a week."

"Thank you," said Joshua. "Now pick this up."

He threw the aluminum can into the pile of expired food and trash and retreated into his room. Donna and Cole picked up the party trash while the snake slithered around on the ground.

CHAPTER SEVENTEEN: BACKSTABBERS

They called the police within hours, but the police were — unsurprisingly but still disappointingly — unhelpful. The hysterical story sounded like this: there were two home-owners and there was a boyfriend, and the boyfriend was overstaying his welcome and so one of the homeowners lost his temper and cut his arm with an aluminum can. It was a classic, boring domestic dispute.

They did come to the house, but everything seemed to cool off at that point. Joshua put on a great show and even bonded with the police about the banality of the issue. At some point, he mentioned the recent death of his mother and that conjured a mess of sympathy. All in all, it was a waste of time.

For the rest of the week, Cole stayed far away. He didn't come over once. He called and gave a whole spiel. The high-lights were, first and foremost, that he felt unsafe there. He couldn't understand why she wasn't going to uproot her life again and leave the house behind. That annoyed Donna. He finished the speech by saying, "I don't want to sleep in the house of someone who cut me with an aluminum can, and you are batshit bananas if you want to continue sleeping there."

* * *

One night, Donna invited herself over to Cole's. She didn't plan to sleep there, per the lawyer Roberta's advice, but she couldn't take his absence any longer. She just wanted to be near him and feel his warmth and his breath and she wanted to argue but she also wanted to make up. It had been quite a while since they'd had sex. Joshua had killed the sensual ambiance around her house. She wanted to be in the honeymoon stage with young, sexy Cole, but instead she was dwelling in the harbor of perpetual anxiety. She also had anxiety about her anxiety. She became afraid that Cole only loved her because of the drama — that he was drawn to it, like a drug. That fear contradicted everything he told her during their argument as he said he wanted simplicity and less drama, but because of Donna's increasingly stressful state, she had a hard time believing anyone, and the truth got tangled up in her mind.

She was paranoid that once her routine settled down and she was back to reality, he wouldn't like her anymore. The irrationality was probably introduced to her mind by Joshua. She worried that if she did do what Cole insisted — bag it all up, escape toxicity — he would be disappointed in her lack of a proper fight. Isn't that what men wanted? Difficult women? Donna was never especially difficult, but there was also never a time she was bored. She was in constant turmoil, even if she didn't show it on the outside. If anything, boring circumstances made her feel the most unsettled. She almost felt more comfortable when something outrageous was going on.

Once upon a time, her boyfriend in Chicago was a little dull and irritating, and she couldn't stand it. Her other internet roommate could have afforded to vacuum more or be less of a shithead. But mainly, she was driven crazy by the two because she wasn't stimulated by them. She didn't know to feel about this trait in herself. She questioned why she wanted to escape the Midwest so badly. If she was so interested in finding herself, then why had she deliberately lost herself?

And per the subject of difficult women, it's possible she enjoyed difficult men. What she hated were absent men. What she didn't mind were men that were pains in the ass. At least they were present. She came to California because she thought it would manifest sunshine and air and light, but somewhere along the way she had almost willingly fallen into a dark hole. California was the coldest, most dreary place on Earth. She was being driven to hysteria, feeling the sexiest and most alive in her body when her mental state was being torn apart. And that reality wrecked her like dynamite at a construction site.

But when Donna arrived at Cole's, he gave her just what she wanted — a seething argument. They fought about how she'd lost her senses and lost touch with herself. She expressed jealousy about the idiosyncrasies of his apartment — how every touch in the place looked "exactly like him." She longed for a place that looked exactly like hers. Before she arrived in California, she never even liked turquoise. She wondered what her favorite color was. Probably the opposite. Probably pink.

His arm still looked gory. It was covered in a small gauze pad and medical tape. It was a strange shape — long and skinny, like a snake. It would likely scar but not badly. Maybe no one would notice it except for Cole and Donna, if he stayed with her. And it would probably live in Joshua's memory forever.

They had it out and then they made up. Donna asked him all kinds of questions about women he had been with in the past. Cole expressed feeling like the conversation was bad timing, but Donna rationalized, "If you want me to uproot my life and give us a chance without the baggage of the house, then you need to be ready for whatever timing of conversation that comes up." Cole commented that she had become bossy in her unhinged state.

Donna told him he didn't know half of it. Then he ripped off her clothes and made love to her. Everything was spinning in a paranormal way. Even though the sex was good, Donna wondered in flashes throughout how she could be having sex when all this uncertainty was going down in her life.

"Kiss me gently but fuck me hard," she said in a bizarre epiphany. "Maybe it's the contrast I crave."

"I don't know what you mean," Cole said. "Do you want to come?"

"No," she said. And she meant it. She was so over-stretched she didn't think her body could bring her there. Like a zombie, she stood up and got dressed and told him she needed to drive home. She didn't want Joshua at the house without her overnight.

* * *

When she returned home, she nearly pissed her pants.

As she drove up, even from the end of the street, she saw the front door of her home had been replaced with a hideous IKEA door, a door that matched the color and shape of the uncharacteristic side door. She parked hastily in a no-parking zone and turned on her hazards. She needed to get to the house fast.

As she got out of the car, a siren booped behind her. She kept walking, zombie-like, toward the house.

"Ma'am?" a cop asked. She kept walking. "Ma'am!" he said, louder.

She was at the door. She tried to jiggle the knob and it was locked. Then, she was banging and screaming for Joshua to let her inside.

"Ma'am," the cop kept talking. "Ma'am, what's going on? What's the problem?"

"I can't get into my house," she said. "The door has been replaced." She walked closer to the cop and his face scrunched, like he noticed something off about her.

"Have you been drinking?" the cop asked.

"No," she said. "I need to get into my house."

"You look a little squiffy," the cop went on. "Are you okay?"

"This was my grandmother's house and she left it to me," she said. "Please, you have to help me. My roommate is dangerous."

"Ma'am, I'm gonna ask you to come with me. I hope you will consent to a breathalyzer. It seems as though you've been driving under the influence."

"Fuck how I've been driving," she said. "My house has been stolen. This is my house."

"If you don't consent to come with me, I'll have to put you in handcuffs," the cop said. "Please."

Donna continued to beat on the door. She was hitting it in full-on punches, screaming at Joshua to open up. "Joshua, please," she shouted. "The police are here, please, just open the fucking door."

"Ma'am," the cop shouted sternly. "Do as I say, please."

She didn't. She kept kicking and punching and kicking and punching.

The cop pulled out a taser and stuck it into her side. Debilitated by shock and pain, Donna fell to the ground.

"Please," she begged. "I need to get into my house."

"I need you to come with me," said the cop. "Lean against the wall."

He pushed her face into the wall of her porch and fastened her hands behind her back. Tears poured down her face. "He replaced the doors," she said.

"Okay, honey," the cop said. "Keep walking."

"He's trying to edge me out," she said. "He wanted this."

"Ex?" the cop asked.

"My roommate," she choked out.

The cop rolled his eyes. "Got it," he said.

When Donna got to the station, it was proven that she had, in fact, been drinking. But she believed that was beyond the point. She had made it safely from point A to point B, had she not? Her only regret was parking in the wrong place in front of the cop. And now, in all the tragedy, she would have to pay for a fucking locksmith once she got back to her place.

CHAPTER EIGHTEEN: THE ATTIC

She wondered what would have happened if she hadn't parked there. If she had parked in a responsible place and made it to her door — her replaced, locked door — and asked the cop for help getting in, would he have helped her? Would he have called her "honey" from the very beginning? She would never know.

Instead, she was charged with a DUI and spent the night in jail. She decided to call her mother before Cole. She would rather die than admit the event to Cole, at least not yet. Even though he dabbled in drinking and driving, he had never been arrested for it. She felt like her behavior was tacky.

Her mother was predictably frustrated but unpredictably angry. But as she told Donna there was no way in fuck she would fly out there to save her from this mess, Donna could hear that she was packing and zipping bags. After her mother berated her for the entirety of the allotted phone call time, she said, "I'll get on the soonest flight I can."

Donna rotted that night in prison. She wished she had more alcohol to at least pass the time and tranquilize her thoughts a bit. She didn't even get on her filthy cot and found the concrete floor cleaner and more comfortable. She had a cellmate, a young girl — only eighteen — who had been arrested for stealing a few hundred dollars' worth of monochromatic desk supplies from Office Max. "I'm a student," she said. "I just wanted my dorm to look cute."

"I wish my mom could bail you out with me," Donna said.

"Would she?" the girl asked, looking hopeful.

"No," Donna said.

"Have you ever been arrested before?" Donna asked.

"No," the girl said. "By God's grace."

The thief girl went to sleep seemingly without a problem while Donna lay eyes-wide and played and replayed the images in her mind — banging on the door and screaming for Joshua, the cop tazing her on her own property, her sweet, sticky alcohol breath.

When Addie finally arrived, it was everything Donna could do to not burst into tears. She immediately purged the whole story — Joshua replaced the doors, she was locked out, humiliated. The ride back to the house was awkward. The rental car smelled like a pine-scented rabbit's foot. No one said anything for a long while, and then finally Addie said, "We need to get him out, Donna. We need to get him out no matter what it costs."

When they arrived back at the house, they called for a locksmith and left a voicemail. It was early in the morning, and they waited for the shop to open in excruciating silence. Donna tried calling Joshua multiple times — the lights in the house were off and her calls went straight to voicemail.

After almost two bleary sun-rising hours, the locksmith arrived, exhausted. "We rarely ever get calls this early," he said, and yawned as he began to work on the door.

Once the door was finally unlocked, Donna held open the door, expecting Addie to walk in. Addie stood stubbornly.

"Aren't you coming in?" Donna asked.

"No. I need to go back home."

"The flight is so long. At least stay for coffee while you make a plan. Take a nap."

"Donna—" Addie started, her face red. "This was very expensive for me. A bailout? And I was supposed to work today."

"I'm sorry," Donna said.

"*Arrested?*" Addie went on. "Are you kidding me? This isn't like you."

"I know," Donna said, ashamed. "Thank you for coming to get me."

"Now I have to fly back across the country and deal with this."

"But what about Joshua?" Donna asked. "You said we need to get him out no matter what the cost."

"Oh, I believe that," Addie said, and bit her lip. "But not today. I need some time. You got yourself into this — I told you it was a bad idea." And then, the worst: "I'm really disappointed in you, Donna." She got back into the car and drove off without hugging her.

* * *

Donna was furious to find that Joshua made a copy of the new door key for her, but it was inside the locked house. It was all one sick manipulative gesture — a game. He wanted her to suffer, and continue to suffer, for as long as she continued to live there. She took the key spitefully and stuck it on her keychain. For now, there was no other option. At around ten in the morning, she heard him leave. He had been in the house the whole time, ignoring her. Maybe he was going to meet with a coworker. Honestly, she didn't care where he went. It wasn't worth her already-thin energy — she needed time alone.

The house was quiet, and she spent the day in muted agony. She called into the salon to lie and say she was sick. It was her first day off in ages, so Lydia was understanding. Donna was far too embarrassed to share the truth. Even though Lydia was her friend, it was important to Donna that Lydia didn't view her any differently.

During the day, she oscillated between a hungover stupor and long naps. By the time it was finally twilight, the day felt even earlier than it had that morning. Her mom sent a passive-aggressive text saying, *Finally made it home. The flight was terrible.*

Donna was too sad to watch television or eat a proper meal. She finally settled on a hot shower and a bag of trail mix. She sat on the shower floor and ate, the peanuts and raisins melting together with warm water in her mouth. Nothing tasted good, but she was dehydrated and needed some semblance of nourishment. She texted Cole and said she'd had a long day. He wrote back and said, *Me too. I hope you're feeling better.* She hoped his long day hadn't been nearly as long as hers — she suspected that it wouldn't have been.

Joshua didn't come home until late, which was a relief. He did send one message mid-afternoon that said, *Just got your calls — Everything okay?* His aloofness made her so angry she almost broke her phone in half. Deciding to be the better person and not respond, she slipped into her favorite PJs and crawled into bed. It was almost peaceful, for a moment. She was clean, her mom was home safe, she had Cole. She knew there had to be an end to Joshua, and soon. But she would save her strategizing for tomorrow, when she was healed, when she was rested.

But just as she almost drifted off to sleep for the night, there was a scratching noise in the wall. It started suddenly and wouldn't stop. Throughout the night, the faint scutter moved up through her walls and in the ceiling. Her first thought was that a squirrel had gotten in and became trapped. Then, she remembered the dark reality she now lived in and suspected the sound was one or more of Joshua's mice.

The next day, when she finally saw him, she asked him about it right away. The door felt like an unsolvable issue that would escalate too quickly for her to tackle now — but the scratching sound maybe had a feasible solution. But Joshua was immediately defensive. He accused her of looking at "any small thing" in his "life habits" that could "ail her."

When she fought back, he fought back harder. She insisted he call an exterminator, but he refused, shouting, "Put it on your tab!" He started to make a myriad of excuses, like how he didn't want any strangers in the house.

"That's how I felt during your stupid fucking birthday party!" she shouted.

"Can't you do anything on your own?" he asked. "Figure out the problem yourself."

"Why would I do that when there are professionals who can do it better?" she scoffed.

"Fine," he said. "If you want to call an exterminator, do it, but I'm not going to contribute to the cost."

"Fine," she shot back. "I'll call one today."

"Whatever," Joshua said. "It's going to be stupidly expensive and he's just going to tell you there are critters — which you already know."

"I don't want critters," she said.

"Spoiled brat," Joshua muttered, and left the house.

Donna took another day off work. The exterminator only took a few hours to arrive.

As it turned out, there was a small family of mice living in the walls. Two must have run off and bred and made a family. Since the baby mice were so young, he suspected the family tree ended there. One nuclear family in the walls, trying their best to escape.

She asked him what to do, what precautions to take. He advised her to go looking in the attic. "I puttered around up there," he said, "but it was hard with all the stuff."

Donna paused at the word "stuff." From what she understood, the attic was empty save for some holiday decorations. That was what her aunts told her when her grandmother died — that they had gone through and separated the valuables from the expendables. Almost nothing of Rudy's was expendable, it turned out, but she also didn't keep an inordinate amount of stuff. There was very little trash, and nothing too cumbersome to move post-death. There was an unusual ease to sorting Rudy's possessions — she was, first and foremost, practical. But she did have a nostalgic streak, one that loved memorabilia. But among that collection, everything was curated, mostly monochrome, handpicked — even in storage boxes in the attic.

"What do you mean stuff?" she asked.

"Oh, you know, there's all that bedding up there. Boxes, suitcases. Looks like a teenager was sleeping up there or something."

"Why would a teenager be sleeping up there?" she asked.

"I don't know," the exterminator said. "For fun? Teenagers are weird." He paused. "Looks like a hoarder lived up there or something."

Donna scoffed. "A hoarder?" she said. "No way."

"You think it's funny," he said. "Some people have a serious problem."

"You think my grandmother had a problem?"

"Or some kid."

"Why do you say some kid?"

"A lot of the trash is like, well, kid snacks."

"Trash?" Donna asked. "Show me."

The exterminator, a stocky, mustached man in a well-fitting cardigan but out-of-style shorts, reached his thick, hobbit-looking hand toward the ceiling and grabbed the tiny attic string. He pulled it down and the ladder lowered, creaking. Small, pink puffs of fiberglass fell to the floor. Fiberglass had always been strange to Donna. She couldn't look at it without imagining it as cotton candy shredding the inside of her throat.

The exterminator began to ascend the stairs. His butt looked silly climbing, and he made oafish sounds as he tried to wedge his sausagey body into the tiny attic entry.

Donna went up with more ease, although she also felt ridiculous. She had no idea what he was describing and expected to see a few boxes, maybe the trash of candy cane wrappers and gingerbread houses.

When they arrived at the top, the light was out. The ceilings were low. It was so bright downstairs during the day, so it took a while for her eyes to adjust. Finally, the exterminator flipped on the light.

Donna was horrified.

* * *

The smell up there was foul. There were bags upon bags of dirty clothes, soiled underwear, snotty rags, sticky paper plates, processed food containers, half-eaten jars of preserves, rotted wood and muddy blankets. There was an abandoned aquarium, with only small traces of water, pebbles and plastic coral spilling out, and the corpses of tiny dead fish sprawled like they were at an archaeological site. There were strange other relics, like a collection of old electronics, hundreds of power cords tangled like necklaces, condom wrappers and used condoms and bloody tissue. Overwhelmingly, there was the smell of urine. All around the ground lay loose batteries and flashlights. In the center, there was an open chest with sentimental-looking children's clothes and toys. There were some well-loved stuffed animals and a selection of embroidered little boys' clothes.

"Yep," said the exterminator, as if he read Donna's mind.

"I had no idea," she gasped, struggling to breath.

"I figured you didn't, based on your reaction," he said.

"This makes so much sense, though," she said. "Sometimes this place smells so bad and I had no idea what it was."

"It's human waste and rotted food and god knows what else."

"How could anyone live like this?"

"I doubt it was your grandmother," he said. "You got any cousins?"

"No," Donna said. "I don't know what or who this could be."

"Well, wasn't she a little, you know, not herself in the end?" Donna's face contorted. The exterminator corrected himself. "I don't mean to pry."

"You're not at all," she said. "I'm sorry. This isn't your business."

The exterminator shrugged.

"My aunts went through and picked up a few things when she died," Donna said. "They didn't see this. They would have told me about it."

"It's possible you had a homeless person living here before you moved in," he said. "Sometimes they find empty places when people pass away." He paused. "Is there anything I can do to help?"

She wanted to take him up on his offer but didn't know what he could do. Plus, she feared the situation was growing further out of her control. She felt determined to find a solution to the issue herself — whether through the law or with Cole and her mother's support. "You've been great," Donna said. "I'm sorry about this."

They awkwardly made their way down the ladder, Donna leading this time, and stood in the foyer. Donna wished him well and tipped him nicely. Before he was about to leave, she caught him. "You know what?" she asked. "Can you give me your phone number?"

The exterminator looked at her dad-like, understanding. "I would be happy to," he said. He pulled out a yellow pad and wrote it down. "I'm Carlo," he said.

"I'm Donna." She paused. "I don't have much family here."

"I live about an hour south in Carson," he said, "with my wife and two kids. Call if you need anything."

She thanked him and watched in a daze as he drove away and faded from her memory. She forgot his mustache, she forgot his pants — he only existed to her in her attic. In all her tension, she quickly misplaced his phone number, which could have been a lifeline. In the turmoil, Donna was increasingly bad at taking help where she needed it.

She thought of all the horrors this house had gone through. The abuse. Why would a homeless person want to live in the attic and not the house as a whole? Since he was already hiding, what more was there to hide?

She went to the kitchen and found a pair of yellow kitchen gloves and a box of trash bags. She wished she had a mask but settled for an old handkerchief to tie around her nose. Then Donna climbed back up into the mysterious attic alone.

* * *

The smell knocked her out even more the second time. The filth stank like a bird had eaten a baby bird and thrown it up. First, she got out her pink Polaroid and took as many photos as possible. Then, she started to go through the trash. If she went through the trash first, she would be able to sort through the personal belongings later. She could see if this had anything to do with her grandmother.

She closed her eyes as she touched the objects and moved them into the garbage. For such a small square footage, the amount of stuff in the attic was impressive. She found tiny spots of creature poop, probably from the mice, and cheap forgotten beer cans.

A lot of the trash was wet. But it was somehow wet and crusted over at the same time. She made her way with the trash but felt like it continued to multiply and pile around her. The smell was so bad she began to think she was hallucinating. She held her breath over and over until her mind went dizzy. She needed water but couldn't imagine ingesting anything. She became afraid she would fall over, through the hole and down the ladder, and break her ankle again.

When she got to the bottom of one corner of trash, she made out the floor beneath. It was rotted wood, as the exterminator said, that looked like it had been eaten by maggots. It was like an old, decayed tree stump that had been covered with peanut butter and devoured by all kinds of grubs. With the stickiness in the room, Donna wouldn't be surprised if at some point this person had caked everything in condiments.

As she cleaned, she revealed a tiny letter box, vintage and blue. It was pretty, still gleaming even in its suspicious sepia glow. It must have belonged to Donna's grandmother. She didn't want to look at the contents here, and she didn't know how much longer Joshua would be out of the house. He was sure to have a barrage of questions Donna wasn't ready to answer. He made everything about him. *His* safety, *his* right to peace, *his* attic. Donna knew that cleaning the attic would be a project for multiple days. She left the cleaning supplies upstairs and grabbed the letterbox. She took it down the ladder and closed the hatch.

Finally in the privacy of her room, Donna poured herself a glass of wine and opened the letter box. It was full of gorgeous stamps, some handwritten letters, and some pictures. There were photos of her grandmother looking vibrant and happy, even in her old age. Then, there were pictures of her when she was sick and started to lose her sparkle.

The letters were personal and intimate — Donna felt guilty rifling through them but remembered she was playing the role of detective. They contained messages from the usual suspects: cousins, sisters, childhood friends. There were several invitations to funerals, probably acquaintances who passed away over the years. At least Donna's grandmother had not been the first to go.

Then, there was a series of photographs held together with a delicate binder clip. In the photos, there was Donna's grandmother looking sick but happy. Each photograph of her had a love note scrawled in cursive on the back — *To Rudy, my ruby* — always the same inscription, penned in blue with the same affection, and dated. The handwriting must have been her boyfriend's. Donna scanned over each portrait and laughed, tears welling in her eyes. There were shots of Rudy on her travels, picking out keychains — the vial of sand Donna kept on her own set of keys. She kept flipping through the stack, unable to take her eyes off her grandmother's face. She looked happy despite everything that was happening with her health. She and this man did so much together. There she was at the movies, at a nice boutique, on a trail through the mountains, the shade on her face, serene.

Looking at the photos, Donna became absorbed by her grandmother's radiance, her unexpired sense of adventure. Given all the portraits, the man had clearly been taken by her. A natural pair. But then, Donna reached the bottom of the stack and found the one picture of them both. Her stomach lurched, and she felt like she was going to be sick. She let out a long moan, animal-like. Her hands started to sweat. Her grandmother's joyful face distorted into an eerie, nightmarish leer.

The man in the picture, the man who had taken care of her and given her joy and all the adventure in the world, was Joshua Flowers.

CHAPTER NINETEEN: DRINKING

Donna hadn't felt so off-balance since the moment she heard her dad had passed away. At the time, she was in middle school, and her friend Eliza was staying over for the night. The girls were in Donna's hot rickety attic room in Norwood Park, Chicago, on a summer night. They were in the process of printing off a conversation they had with Eliza's crush on AOL Instant Messenger. They didn't want to forget a single moment — it was one of their first flirtations. The printout of this document would go on to be something Donna never got rid of. It sat folded forever in her yearbook from that year, sitting in a closet in her mother's basement, memorializing the exact moment Donna learned of her father's passing.

Addie was downstairs having a glass of wine with their neighbor lady when the house phone rang. It was Rudy who broke the news. At first, Donna and Eliza heard a faint commotion but brushed it off. But as things escalated, Addie began to shout and then wail, then the neighbor lady yelled to the girls to come downstairs.

"He died," Addie cried, and Donna knew exactly who she meant. It was the first time she felt the universe close in on her, truly — her father, who didn't seem to care much for her existence at all — had died of colon cancer, and he hadn't even bothered to tell anyone about it. There, it was written in the sand then that he would never be able to make up for those lost years.

Rather than feeling upset, she was overcome with rage. Why hadn't he called her? Why didn't even Addie know he had been ill? From a young age, she learned it was possible to feel utter disdain for someone who was dead. The printout of the AIM conversation meant more to her in the end than his funeral bulletin or even the sorry amount of money he left her in his will. The AIM conversation was the symbol of who she was before and who she was after.

The pictures of Rudy with Joshua Flowers evoked a similar reaction in Donna. Like the vague details of her father's death, the photographs of Rudy and Joshua's vacations proved that Joshua was full of malice. He didn't have a hot temper. He didn't deserve forgiveness for going through grief with his mom. He was a chronically conniving person with a terrifying agenda. At that moment, she decided she didn't really know anything about this person. For all she knew, every word Joshua had ever spoken to her was untrue. It was a Craigslist nightmare. He was the former caretaker and lover of her grandmother, and he had been in the house all along.

Donna was too furious to do anything for what felt like several hours.

She thought of all his stuff up there — the strange hoarder tendencies he had hidden from her. His room was mysteriously barren and clean, then remodeled into a spa. She thought of his taste and his cooking ability and his hospitality. And worst of all, she thought of his charisma and all the qualities she had adored about him, like their initial natural banter. She wondered if these traits were the things her grandmother had adored, too. Or if he had been a different man then. If he had shown her somebody different.

When she was finally able to move again, she wondered if he was home now. In her shock, she couldn't process anything around her. She was paralyzed in blackness, in the twisting, curling, thorning vines of her mind. In the center of it all, she felt betrayed. Here was a man who she'd once called a friend.

She stood at her bedroom window. She was overwhelmed, even in the complete silence. The sound of empty air hurt her ears. A pit of loneliness swelled in her gut. She convinced herself no one understood her, no one could empathize with her pain. Her feelings toward Joshua bordered on infatuation. She was heartbroken for reasons she didn't understand. It was like she had a lover and lost him.

She called her Aunt Sheeba and asked to go visit her as soon as possible.

* * *

The drive to Thousand Oaks was dangerous, and traffic was terrible. Donna was drinking, despite her altercation with the police. Her license was on a six-month suspension, but she was feeling too low to care. She stopped at the liquor store and got three large cans of hard seltzer. She hoped if people passed her on the road, they wouldn't be able to tell what it was. They looked like energy drinks, at least that's what she told herself, so she felt discreet as she drank and drove. Still, her driving became more and more spotty.

To her disgust, it was a lovely day. As she drove, she remembered why she had wanted to move to California. This was it: these were the coasts and the waters and the lifestyle. There was the sun and the sky and the expansive green cliffs. There was her freedom. But hanging over it was something she had not anticipated, a crushing mountain of dread and sorrow. She hated California. She hated it as she had never hated anything before. It was a miserable place filled with miserable people. She hated herself and her job and her expectations. Why had she thought it would be helpful for her to relocate? All relocating did was magnify the parts about herself she already hated in the Midwest.

She was still lazy, she told herself. Largely incompetent, and too much of a dreamer to get much of anything done.

She lived in a fantasy. She had trouble connecting to people. She played too nice. She was a pushover. And she was still cold, god damnit, no matter how warm it was outside, she always felt cold.

She pulled over when her drunkenness made her eyes bleary. She stood at the edge of a cliff and screamed. With every bit of new information regarding Joshua Flowers, she became less close to understanding him. Every new puzzle piece opened a new conundrum. To know him was to work backwards, all the time. So she centered her thoughts and tried to start from the beginning: what had she liked about him when she first met him?

She couldn't think of anything.

She realized she hadn't liked him especially but liked who she was with him. He made her feel like a leader for a moment — like someone who had the reins on her own shit. She associated him with the early days of California — the bike, the new hair, the chance to be a-fucking-way from her uniform life for once.

Sure, he had his quirks which led to charms which led to curiosities. Then, the curiosities had deepened. Why was he so strange? Why was he so particular? Why did his peculiarities, no matter how far from Donna's peculiarities they were, make her feel so understood? It was the weirdness itself, rather than the contents of the weirdness, that made her feel seen. In understanding Joshua's weirdness, Donna had embraced the weirdness of herself. She had a comrade. She had him, she had him, and then he was gone.

She fell asleep on the cliff in the open air, resentful of how Joshua was making her hit rock bottom as a human. How dare he cause her to be the sort of person who drinks and drives, who pulls over on the side of the road to pass out. How dare he?

She awoke at around four in the morning. The sun wasn't far from rising. Her pocket was vibrating to the rhythm of Aunt Sheeba's phone calls. She was crazily worried, naturally. The thirty-minute drive had extended into the early morning.

Donna hopped in the car, still a quarter drunk, and finished the journey to Thousand Oaks. When she arrived, her aunt was waiting on the porch with a lot of battering comments. The first being, "What the hell were you thinking? I thought you'd had an accident on the road." And then, "Get inside."

When Donna did, in fact, get inside, she wasn't sure where to begin. She felt broken, like she was going through a breakup. Aunt Sheeba was so far removed from the issue with her grandmother and the mysterious man. Instead, she thought Donna was going through a breakup with Cole.

"Geographically, I know I'm your closest family member," she sympathized, "so I am willing to help you through this time." But before Donna could get a word in, she said, "But I have to be honest, Donna, I have a lot going on in my own life and I'm not sure how much heartspace I can dedicate to your shenanigans."

Before Donna got defensive, she realized her behavior did warrant the description of shenanigans. Not long before, she had been passed out drunk on the side of a highway.

"I'm sorry, Aunt Sheeba," she said.

"I don't want you to say you're sorry. I want to know you're all right."

"Well, I'm not."

"What did he do?" Aunt Sheeba had the look of female family solidarity, like she would gladly show up at Cole's place with a pickaxe and hack out his brain.

Donna told her no, things with Cole were okay — although not great —that the person in question was Joshua.

"Who?" Aunt Sheeba asked, confused. "Are you dating someone else?"

"No, Sheeba, Joshua. My roommate."

"Your roommate?"

Donna pulled out the photograph. Of Joshua, and her grandmother, looking radiant.

"That's Davey!" Aunt Sheeba exclaimed. "Where did you find this?"

"In the attic," Donna said. "And that isn't Davey. It's Joshua."

Aunt Sheeba stared at her. "I'm confused."

"Me, too. This man in the picture isn't called David, at least not to me. This man is my roommate."

Aunt Sheeba stared at her for another moment before getting up and leaving the room for some time. Donna expected she would come back with a tea or something to snack on. But when she came back, she had a pen and paper and a chain with reading glasses around her neck.

"What are you doing?" Donna asked.

"I want to know everything," Sheeba said, ready to take notes. "Go on — we have to figure all this out."

CHAPTER TWENTY: MASLOW'S HIERARCHY OF NEEDS

After Aunt Sheeba forcefully signed herself on as co-detective, Donna head home. The women were in close contact via email and when Joshua left, Donna took Polaroids of everything in the house she could — his bedroom, the backyard, the *ABA Journals*. She went to an office supply store and bought a miniature scanner to run through the Polaroids and send them off to Sheeba. Sheeba responded with everything she could manage to scrape up — letters from Rudy's travels with Joshua, a couple of voicemails detailing her love affair, and even hospital records that documented discharges of Rudy in Joshua's care.

Donna didn't know where the evidence was leading, but as Roberta had suggested, they were building a case. After a while, Donna got used to Aunt Sheeba's irksome tendencies — every time they were on the phone, she crunched ice directly into the receiver — but as some days went on, Donna began to look forward to their conversations. They were so involved with their project she even had some distraction from her problems with Cole.

Quickly, Donna's desire for Joshua Flowers to leave surpassed the meaning of desire — it became a need. She could no longer survive knowing he inhabited her house. She had to ensure his removal.

In her pursuit of evidence, she reached out to Joshua's brother, Gabriel, first. He was pleasantly surprised to hear from her. So much so that Donna felt afraid to break the bad news.

"Where are you right now?" she asked him, hesitantly.

"I'm at home," Gabriel said. "Why? What's going on?"

"Do you have a minute?"

Gabriel paused. "Yes. But I have a feeling this will take longer than a minute."

"Listen," Donna said, "I don't want to stir the pot with you, Gabriel. You seem nice, but there are some things that have happened with Joshua that I thought his family should be aware of."

"Okay . . ." Gabriel trailed off. "I'm listening."

"I know life must be tough," Donna went on, "with your mother passing away."

"I'm sorry. My mother?"

Donna didn't know what to say.

Thankfully, Gabriel kept talking. "Listen, Donna, I'm not sure if you're clear about this, but Joshua isn't my brother. We just call each other family. We're chosen family."

"I'm sorry." Donna's stomach lurched. "What?"

"Yeah," Gabriel said. "I've only known Joshua a few years. He wasn't doing so hot when I met him, so we kinda formed a special bond."

"What is a chosen family?"

"Um . . . this puts me in a weird situation," Gabriel said.

"Why?"

"We're sort of, um, bound to secrecy. It's a loyalty thing." He took a few breaths, and Donna heard him drink a sip of a beverage. "You really don't know how Joshua and I met?"

"Obviously not," she said. "I thought you were brothers."

"No," Gabriel said. "Well, we are, in a way." He sighed and took another sip. "Is everything okay?"

"No," Donna said.

"But is Joshua safe?" Gabriel asked.

"What? Yes, he's safe. What's going on?"

"I will tell you how I met him, but you have to promise me you won't disclose it to Joshua, okay? I just want to tell you because it seems as though there's been a major misunderstanding," he said.

"I promise," Donna said, her fingers halfway crossed.

"I was his probation officer," Gabriel said.

"Probation from what?"

"He was in prison," Gabriel went on. She stopped breathing. "Donna?"

She didn't know what to say.

"It made me so happy to see how well he's doing out there, with the house and the bedroom and the pet and everything . . . are you okay?"

"What was he in prison for?" she asked.

"He was squatting in someone else's house," he said, "and things got really out of hand."

"Where?"

"Funny enough," Gabriel said, "If I remember correctly, it was his brother. His actual brother. Not me. It evolved into a domestic dispute, dragged on for months. He never actually laid hands on anyone, but he did threaten to hurt his sister-in-law. That was enough to get him in pretty bad trouble. He spent six months in jail because they found weapons in his possession, so the threat seemed viable. Anyway, I was assigned to him to get his life back on track. And it seems like he did. But you're saying his mother died?"

"She shot herself." Donna was brash. "In a horse stable."

"Good Lord," Gabriel said. "I'm sorry to hear about that. I should reach out to him."

"No need," Donna said. "I'm starting to realize he isn't trustworthy at all." She began to tear up a little bit. "He is squatting in my house, too."

"Has he been violent?" Gabriel asked.

"Yes."

He took a long, tired pause. "Donna, you need to report this."

"I tried."

"He has a record."

"I know that now."

"Can you help me?" she asked.

"You know what," Gabriel said. "I want to, but I'm not in that field anymore."

"Can you help me as a friend?"

Gabriel paused and thought and thought. "No," he said. "I'm sorry. I'm trying to distance myself from that whole life." Donna wanted to scream. Then why the fuck had he come to the party? Aunt Sheeba was going to be outraged when she heard about this. "Joshua was one of my last assignments," Gabriel went on. "I was curious to see how he was doing, and I think I needed that closure that I helped someone and did something right."

"You didn't though," Donna said sharply. "Because nothing has changed, and you won't even do anything to help me."

Gabriel sighed a long breath. "This is why I wanted to leave that life, Donna," he said. "This isn't the first time I've gotten a call like this — not just about Joshua, but about everyone. It's taxing, after a while. This isn't my fault."

Donna wanted to be sympathetic but couldn't. How dare he side with a criminal? Before she hung up the phone, she asked, "What about the other woman who was here?" Donna demanded. "Iona. Was that really his sister?"

"No," Gabriel said. "It was another woman in the program."

"She called him brother, too."

"Well, she's an ex-con," he said. "Maybe she was in on it."

"Jesus Christ," Donna said, frustrated. She hung up and slammed down the phone. Moments later, it rang again.

"Joshua Flowers isn't his real name," Gabriel said. "It's Donovan Sandoval." Then, he hung up.

Donna sat with this new information. She considered calling his alleged sister but felt she wouldn't be any help — plus she was also dangerous, apparently. In any case, it seemed like everyone who knew Joshua didn't actually know him, and that was disappointing. It was also disappointing because the face Joshua presented to society was a nice face. Grandma Rudy loved him. Donna loved him. He could radiate with a positive spirit that seemed to fit right in. He fit in. He was nice when he wanted to be. He was everything when he wanted to be.

* * *

Donna reported the new information to Aunt Sheeba, who relished it. The trouble with Sheeba, Donna thought, was that she was having too much fun solving the case to such an extent that sometimes her profound enthusiasm halted tangible progress. But Donna continued to include her so she could indulge in her curiosity — plus, she was grateful for the information Sheeba had provided. The case against Joshua was at least building momentum.

In the bungalow, Donna didn't sleep for days, which brought her into a disoriented, euphoric state. She worked tirelessly on the case and felt black-eyed and hideous, but the purple bags under her eyes brought her a certain level of glamour. She wasn't the radiant California girl. She was the troubled California girl, a black hole surrounded by sunshine.

To protect her privacy, she made most of her investigation emails and calls from the salon, after hours. The last thing she needed was Joshua snooping in and getting more steps ahead of her. She was uncomfortable with him lurking around under the same roof as her, but for now he was subdued. She suspected he was plotting something, but she enjoyed the temporary lack of action.

She tried to stay productive but struggled to wrestle away the feeling that all the wrong in her life was her fault. Sometimes she spiraled, feeling she could do no right, couldn't take care of a home, and couldn't protect herself. Because of her, her boyfriend had been slashed in the arm. Because of her, her grandmother's home was doomed. Under her watch, the attic above her head had been destroyed by human waste and secrets.

Donna spared Cole the ongoing details to protect him from the drama, as he requested. "Figure it out," he had told her, "or at least figure a fraction of it out — and whenever you call me, I will be here."

She knew she couldn't fully be with him until she rid herself of Joshua — but how and when she would get rid of him was still a plan in progress. She felt stubborn about staying in the house. She wanted to stay in her bedroom, in the walls that were still holding up and, in some ways, protecting her.

She overheard Joshua on the phone telling someone the snake wasn't eating and, after a quick Google, she learned the snake was probably starving himself to eat a nice, warm, large meal. She hoped the meal would be Joshua but feared it would be her.

The side door kept featuring in her dream. The door reminded her of an escape, she rationalized. It wasn't the escape she expected, but it was the one she had to take. She fantasized about packing up the essentials and leaving through that door and never looking back. She could live in her car or on the beach. She could live on a pile of rocks in a cave. She could live inside her dark, drunken mind.

CHAPTER TWENTY-ONE: HOT BATH

Donna pulled all she had from her savings account to send her mother money for a flight back out to California. They weren't necessarily friends again, but as Aunt Sheeba put it, "Once she sees our case, she won't be able to refuse."

When Addie said they needed to get Joshua out at whatever the cost, Donna took her word for it. So late one evening at the salon, she forwarded one big ZIP file to her mother that contained all the evidence she had gathered: photographs, letters, voicemail MP3s, hospital discharges, and everything else relevant. Then, she sent her a QuickPay for the cost of a flight out with the memo, "Please come now."

Within moments, Addie called Donna — first, she was concerned for Donna's safety. Second, she was impressed by Donna's sleuthing. "You did this all by yourself?" she asked.

Donna wanted to tell her mom about Aunt Sheeba, but because of the distance between Addie and her ex-husband's family, she decided to keep it to herself. "It's been a lot of work," she answered, indirectly. "So what do you say?"

"Well, I have to come out," Addie said, barely masking her excitement and concern. "I need to tell my boss I'll be working remotely for a while." Donna was surprised. Her mom was a bookkeeper and rarely took time off work. She heard Addie clicking around on the computer, searching for flights, talking to herself. "This is an urgent situation if I ever heard one."

* * *

Two days later, Donna and her mother reconvened at an unassuming taproom on the side of the road. They weren't in a very friendly-seeming neighborhood, but it was far enough away from the bungalow in Topanga to not run into Joshua. The gray sky made the wooden side walls of the decrepit taproom building seem damp. Donna's mother wasn't much of a beer drinker, so the divey choice surprised Donna, but the transformation of the two to seedy citizen detectives was also riveting. But then, on-brand, Addie ordered a gin and tonic.

"I need something to light me up a bit," Addie said.

"I'll have an IPA," Donna chimed in at the bartender. "Whatever's on tap."

"This is outrageous, Donna," her mother said, jumping right in. "I don't believe any of it."

"Well, believe it," said Donna. "It's real and it's all I've thought about for weeks."

The bartender put down their drinks and Donna's mother opened a tab. "We're gonna need more," she said in an abnormally defensive tone.

"Lady," the bartender replied, "You don't gotta explain nothing to me."

Where the fuck were they? Donna wondered. Everyone in the bar looked like plastic jewelry, gaudy people pretending to be rich. They probably thought they were much closer to Hollywood than they were.

After a moment of taking in the scenery and each other's presence, Addie leaned in and whispered, "I have a gun, Donna."

She stared at her mother for a moment. "Where the fuck did you get a gun?"

"Shh. I've always had a license," she said.

"Not in California, you don't," Donna said.

"I got it at a small shop on the side of the road," Addie went on. "On the way here."

"Oh my god, this country," Donna said, downing her drink.

"We gotta get him out of that place," Addie said.

Donna was embarrassed and annoyed and angry at her mother all at once, but also admired her gall. She felt grateful for her two closest family members — Sheeba, a ruthless investigator, and Addie, an accomplice.

The pair began to strategize how to confront Joshua. After days of his heavy silence, Donna was ready to rile him up.

* * *

When they drove up to the bungalow, they were both a little buzzed and out of sorts. Donna didn't think her mother was aware of how dangerous Joshua could be, and Addie didn't think Donna was aware of how much she didn't give a fuck. If anything, the last twenty-four hours had brought her more excitement than she had in years. She was ready for an epic debacle.

The house was lit dimly behind the beautiful trees. When they got out of the car, ready for a fight, they hesitated in its beauty. "It really is a gorgeous house," Donna's mother said.

Donna expected her mother to move carefully and gingerly, but instead she watched in shock as her mother marched up to the door, twisted the lock, and stepped inside.

Joshua was nowhere to be found, but the snake was resting peacefully on the sofa. There was a bag of chips nearby and the television was on, like the snake was relaxing watching *Cutthroat Kitchen*.

The two women made eye contact and shared a questioning expression. It didn't seem like anyone was home — the bathroom light was off and Joshua's bedroom door was closed. They crept over and placed their ears to it. It seemed quiet.

The shadowy house smelt strongly of incense. It did not make Donna feel more comfortable.

Donna's mother went to the kitchen and began to inspect for any evidence of Joshua while Donna went to the side door, opened it and crept into the backyard. The grass looked worse than ever, patchy and unruly at once, like a person going ungracefully bald.

When she re-entered the living room, the snake was gone and she heard a faint sound in the bathroom. She made her way into the cracked door and found Joshua in a robe, sitting on the side of the bathtub.

"Hi," he said calmly.

"Did you hear us come in?" she asked.

"I did." He looked to Donna's mother. "I'm Joshua."

"I'm aware," she said. "I need you to get out of this house before I call the police."

"No, thank you," he said with a shrug. Donna saw the snake had moved from its position on the couch and was slithering along the edge of the bath. Its slow, calculated movements gave her the same shivers as Joshua's coldness.

"Did you bring your mom in for moral support?" he asked. "To get me out?"

"Actually, yes." Addie stepped in.

Joshua ignored her. "Hasn't California been a disappointment to you?" he asked Donna. "Nothing has really happened for you here."

"A lot has happened for me here," Donna said. "I got that great job, I got a boyfriend. Plus I'm in fucking California, okay? What could be better?" She felt stupid saying it, but it was her truth.

"If you always wanted it, then why didn't you come out and care for that poor woman?" he asked. He put his foot in the hot water of the bath. "None of you took care of her. I did."

"Listen," Donna's mother snapped. "You lied to her the entire time."

"I loved her," said Joshua. "I loved her so much. And I want to keep loving her by keeping up with what she would have wanted. Which is me, in her house. I think Rudy brought us together, Donna."

"She did not bring us together," Donna said, raising her voice now. At the sound of her stress, the snake swirled back around the toilet and started inching toward her.

"Yes, she did," Joshua insisted. "When I heard you on the phone with your mom, ready to post on Craigslist, I thought it was too good to be true. I'd been up in the attics for weeks, then I saw that I had an actual in."

Donna felt momentarily repulsed by the idea of Joshua living above her, listening to her conversations. "Yeah, I found your disgusting hideaway up there," Donna said. "How could you live like that?"

Joshua pouted his lower lip, in mocking sympathy. "It wasn't ideal, but I knew it wouldn't be long," he said. "I knew you wouldn't last one year alone."

The snake, now at Donna's feet, started to coil slowly around her leg. If he constricted her there and then, Donna wouldn't much mind. She was done. She hated everything.

Donna's mother suddenly flashed her gun. "If you don't get the snake off my daughter, I will kill it."

"Okay," said Joshua. "Kill it, then."

"What's the matter with you?" Donna's mother shot back. "Really, I want to know."

"My mother just died," he said. "I've been really down."

"Besides that," she said. "Besides fucking that. What was the matter with you when you decided to move into this place, to manipulate Rudy and trash the attic? What was the matter with you when you agreed to pay your rent and then bailed? What's the matter with you now? Sitting there acting like a fucking creep. Tell me. What."

Donna felt the snake tighten around her ankle a little bit. It was the ankle she had broken earlier in the year — as if it hadn't been through enough already.

"I bet you wish you knew me," Joshua said calmly. "I bet you wish you could know me so deeply."

"I thought I did know you," Donna said. She reached into her pocket and pulled out the picture of Joshua with her grandmother. "When I look at this picture," she said, "I see a picture of my friend with my grandmother. I still have a hard time separating your good and your evil."

Joshua ignored her. "May I ask you both to leave the room, so I can get in the bath?" he asked. "You know, modesty and all."

The snake tightened around her leg, moving slowly up her body. Donna brought her arm down to pull him off, but he was too strong. She started to feel dizzy and couldn't believe the strength in his thin body.

Joshua looked down at her leg, "Donna," he said. "Donna, you might want to move."

"Help me," Donna said. She was terrified. "Help me, please." She slumped down onto the floor.

Addie turned to Joshua, panic and fury all over her face. "How do we get it off her?" she demanded.

"I don't know," said Joshua. He surprisingly looked a little panicked, too. "I don't know."

"Guys," Donna said, the snake squeezing her tighter. "Do something!"

Joshua reached his hand for the gun and snatched it. Addie tried to stop him, but it was too late. Would he kill them? Would he take the gun and run? But instead, he pointed it at the snake's belly, a portion that was centimeters close to Donna's leg, and fired. The snake let out a loud hiss and let go instantly, its twenty-foot body falling backwards. From the end of its tail, the thing rose as tall as it could — the top of its head hitting the ceiling. It scaled the wall in fear and pain.

Then Joshua fired another shot, right at its head. The room splattered with blood and brain matter and teeth. A sprinkle of hard teeth fell to the ground in clinks, like bracelet beads.

Joshua placed the gun back on the bathroom counter, where Addie quickly intercepted it. Donna caught her breath and wiped her face of sweat. When she looked at her hand, there were specks of blood. Her mother stood silent, in disbelief. Donna rolled onto her stomach and put her head in her hands and began to sob. Joshua Flowers had saved her life, he had saved her from being constricted and devoured by a snake, by his own snake, but it didn't make her indebted to him.

Joshua turned off the bathwater.

"Your bath," Donna's mother said, which was the most instinctual and motherly thing she could have said.

"Never mind that," said Joshua.

He led them into the common area and opened a bottle of wine. Donna's leg was throbbing. Without a word, Joshua presented the two women with glasses and poured one for himself. They all sat in silence and drank the wine, blood on each of their faces.

Addie looked especially wrecked, a blob of snake brain goop matting down her hair.

"The snake," said Donna.

"I don't care," Joshua said. "I got him mostly to scare you."

Donna face palmed in frustration. "Are you kidding?"

"I was so jealous when you got this place, Donna, and look what's happened."

"I am afraid of you," she said to Joshua. "Are you even aware of the trauma you've caused?"

"No," said Joshua. "It really isn't a big deal. Just a year out of your life."

Addie's mouth gaped open as widely as it possibly could. "A year out of our lives?" she said. "What happens when you don't leave this place? What happens when we can't get rid of you?"

"You'll find a way," he promised. "They all do."

CHAPTER TWENTY-TWO: CHOSEN FAMILY

Donna went to her next salon shift early and looked up Joshua's real brother. It didn't take too much effort. She ran a police record search for Donovan Sandoval and he came up easily. Their faces were similar, and she realized how stupid she was for trying to see a resemblance between Joshua and Gabriel.

Joshua's real brother, Ricky, almost hung up the phone when Donna mentioned the call was about his brother. "I have a restraining order," he said. "I don't want to talk about him ever again."

"I'm in your shoes," said Donna. "He is here. And he will not leave."

Ricky sighed. "I don't know what to tell you. I lost my wife because of him, I lost access to seeing my kid, I lost my job. He drove me mad. He sucked me dry and took everything I had. He left me out to hang dry in a storm."

"To me, his name is Joshua. Joshua Flowers."

"I'm sorry for you," he said. "If you push him far enough, he'll act out," Ricky promised. "It's what I had to do. I pushed him so hard he threatened my life. Just don't go too far . . . could be fatal."

Donna could feel him itching to get off the phone. "One last thing," she said. "Can you tell me more about your mother?"

"I don't know what you mean," Ricky said. "We haven't seen that woman since we were kids." Just as Donna suspected. Ricky continued, "When we were kids, he used to self-mutilate," he said, rather clinically. "Like, all the time. When this or that would come up, he'd carve the inside of his thighs like they were a custom engraved wood panel. It was his way of getting attention. I think when he was done with himself, he moved onto other people. He's never known how to feel appreciated in the right ways."

Donna didn't want Joshua to feel appreciated at all. Every single thing he ever told her was not true. Except, maybe, that he liked rosé and charcuterie boards. But of even that, she couldn't be sure.

* * *

Donna and her mother stayed in a motel near Rudy's house. After the unsettling killing of the snake, they needed some space away from Joshua. The motel looked like a sex dungeon with red walls and yellowy fabrics. On the ground, there spread an unsightly gold plush rug with glitter stuck in the fabric. Because of the state of the room, Donna's mother had no guilt smoking indoors.

"I wish you wouldn't do that," Donna said.

"Either shut your mouth or join me," her mother said.

Donna accepted the offer and lit one for herself. She walked to the window and stared out at the car. She wanted to resolve all this but also had the urge to just leave with her mom and go back to Chicago. She knew she couldn't escape everything. She had worked this hard so far and committed to making a plan.

"Ricky says if he pushed him hard enough, he would give in," Donna said. "But what would push him?" she thought aloud. "Every little thing I did to go after him didn't bother him much at all."

"Nothing?" Donna's mother asked. "You didn't do anything that you thought just really kicked him in the nuts?"

"No," said Donna, defeated.

"It's so unfair," her mom said. "How is he so calm?"

"I don't know," said Donna. "But he's calm until he's not." She thought about the episode with Cole, when Cole was throwing away the contents from the fridge.

She had an epiphany.

"I got it," she said.

Donna's mother leaned forward, interested. She bit her lip — the mother-daughter crime duo were onto the next lead.

"He got really upset about food," Donna said. "He freaked out when Cole was throwing away his food. That was why he cut him with the aluminum can."

"Food . . ." Donna's mother tapped her cigarette into an old coffee cup. The window reflected in her eyes. "I'm not surprised."

"Why not?"

"Sounds like his mama wasn't there," she said. "Sounds like mama wasn't feeding her babies. Or housing them properly. Everyone's gotta eat."

"Yeah," Donna agreed, deep in thought. "Yeah, they do."

* * *

In the morning, Donna returned to the house and was surprised to find the door was the same, unlocked. It felt unexpectantly peaceful inside.

For a moment, alone in the space, she imagined what Rudy must have felt like in this house. It was her pride; it was the only thing she held close to her. While she was detached from her family and didn't have many close friends, the house reflected her very soul. Donna was curious about the other contents of this soul — the secret parts, the parts that only Rudy knew, the parts that died with her.

She was surprised to find the blood had been cleaned up. The dishes were done, and the floor partially swept. Details were missed, like the curtains were not properly tied back and the pillows looked squashed. Stretched long, all the way twenty feet long, was the decapitated snake's body. He was laid by the back door, like a casual reminder to take out the trash. She thought about the things people take out with the trash: apple cores, empty beer bottles . . . giant snake skins.

She tiptoed closer to the snake and looked into its blown-up face. She felt pity. This thing was bred to constrict and devour. It was his job. He had just been doing his job, better than she ever did any of hers. Her ankle was badly bruised and, now, looking at the carcass, she couldn't believe its strength. Without its life source, it seemed so delicate — a long, leathery necklace.

Her mother had begged to come with her that morning, but Donna thought it best to work alone, at least for a little while. She wanted to confront her fears head-on. The snake was her first fear, and Joshua had taken care of it. Her second fear was Joshua, and she needed to overcome him.

The women agreed the best way to get to Joshua would be to make his vitality seem in jeopardy. But not through threats or physical games. The best way to get to Joshua might be to make him feel as though his basic needs were deprived: food, shelter, and most of all, love.

If he didn't have access to these necessities, he may be reminded of his mother. His mother whom he had killed psychologically, by making a false memory of her shooting her face off in a horse stable. She must have been a terrible mother, Donna considered, reflecting on what Ricky had said about how she wasn't even around most of their lives.

Donna did wonder about his mother on a personal level and the mysteries of her troubled past. She wondered how someone could give birth to three children and then just not care about them. But then Donna thought of all the things she took on that she didn't care about — boyfriends, jobs, hairstyles, coffee mugs. If she was deterred by these choices that were so low commitment, she couldn't imagine being deterred by a family that would take over her very existence.

To her delight, Joshua was not home. She felt he must have expected her to come and needed to evacuate. Or maybe he left the house open for play. Maybe he wanted a little game where Donna could find ways to get at him. Because of this, Donna was certain: Joshua Flowers was miserable. Whether he intended to or not, he was practically waving a flag that begged someone to yank him away from his sadness.

She thought the best place to go would be back to the attic to further analyze the contents of Joshua's life, so she unfolded the ladder and braced herself to climb up. For a moment, she imagined what she looked like from a bird's eye view — as if, for some reason, the camera was looking down on her from inside the attic as she came up. She wondered how her face looked. Horrified? Exhausted? Bewildered?

When the lights flipped on, she saw a small mouse scurry into the darkness. The trash she began to bag on her last excursion remained where she had left it, and the place looked like when she first came upon it — desperate, secretive, sad.

First, she encountered a large gallon Ziploc bag labeled "Rudy." Inside, there were a few sentimental items of her grandmother's. There was a hair ribbon, a few samples of perfume, several rubber band-bound stacks of letters and a picture of Joshua. The picture was labeled "David, my friend" and dated a few months before her death. Alongside the picture, there was a list of songs. The list contained ambiguous love songs — songs that seemed to be written for a friend but were encrypted with passion and longing. She wondered who had compiled the playlist. Maybe it was Joshua, maybe it was Rudy.

Donna thought about how her grandmother hadn't really known Joshua at all, and that broke her heart. For a moment, she thought, "She didn't know him like I know him," but then Donna paused and remembered she didn't know much about him at all either.

In the corner, somewhere beneath a pile of seemingly unused skis and tennis equipment, there was a package sealed with tape labeled "Mom."

CHAPTER TWENTY-THREE: MOM

The package was wrapped in a simple white shoestring. She pulled the shoestring delicately and placed it in a perfect line beside her. The shape reminded her of the snake. She tried to shake the memory of the dead animals from her mind and stay focused. It was only a matter of time before Joshua arrived back home. Surely, he knew Donna must be searching through the place. Still, he couldn't be so gracious as to offer her the luxury of an entire afternoon.

At the top of the Ziploc, there was a fragile object wrapped in a scarf. The scarf smelled of a buttery perfume — one of the savory kinds not many people were drawn to. There was nothing sweet about it, yet it smelled like a baked good. Like fresh bread. Like warmth. The scarf was a red silk square, patterned in flowers of a different shade of red. It brought Donna great pleasure to hold it and smell it. She had to actively remind herself that the person who had owned it would not have brought her — or Joshua — such comfort.

Inside the scarf, there was a ceramic coffee cup. The cup was plain white, and "Best Mom Ever" was printed across it in black courier font. At the rim of the glass was a perfect kiss of lipstick. Donna smelled the inside of the mug and realized the mug had not been washed since its last use. For just a second, her heart broke for Joshua's inherent sentimentality. Then, she knocked sense back into herself and placed the mug and the scarf to the side and continued.

Beneath that, there was a handful of dried lavender. It was wrapped in a tiny black bow. It looked like something his mother must have received as a gift or used as a decoration. Next to that, there was a picture of Joshua and Ricky and a girl, whom Donna presumed to be Joshua's sister, as teenagers. Beneath the photo, there were several empty bottles of airplane-sized liquors. They were mostly Jack Daniels, but there were one or two vodkas in the mix. Donna wondered why these objects had made it into the box. Beneath that, there was a fur that still smelled of animal. Authentic.

And beneath that was a major highlight of the package, a letter addressed to Donovan, Richard and Melanie. The letter was a long apology that detailed a few events that led Joshua's mother to leave the children behind. Donna read over the events in heartache — she couldn't imagine being left by her mother at such a young age. Some of the events included overbearing tendencies of Joshua's father. He screamed at her in public spaces, worked to undermine her in the home, and created a generally embarrassing set of scenarios that caused Joshua's mother to lose all her friends. The whole thing was ghastly — based in truth of real events but dripping with mental instability. Most of all, it seemed as though Joshua's mother just couldn't handle her feelings. She was gaslit for too many years and, as a result, too disturbed to function. In one sentence she wrote, "I never thought I could be driven from my own children, but it seems as though I loathe you all now, too."

Beneath that, in parentheses, it said, "I love you behind the loathing."

The parenthetical made Donna feel as if she were going to be sick. It was like her love for her family was an afterthought, but after studying the letter again and again, Donna realized it was the thing that bound Joshua's mother together. She loved her family so much that it allowed her to feel a crippling amount of pain. The pain didn't allow her to remain with them as long as she wanted to or could have.

Under the letter, there was another document written by Joshua in children's handwriting. The document was titled "Hunger" and it seemed to be an essay written for class. In the margins, the teacher had written, "Donovan, I think it would be helpful to have a meeting with me and you and your parents. Can you have your parents sign this paper and bring it back to class?"

The letter was unsigned. Still, Donna wondered if the meeting between the four had ever happened. Based on how everything turned out, she assumed it had not.

"Hunger" was a short story about a little boy whose parents kept food in their bedroom, away from the common areas. In the story, the little boy's food was rationed during his mealtimes, and when mealtimes were over, he was restricted from access to food. In the first few paragraphs of the essay, the choice seemed somehow innocuous. It seemed as though the little boy's parents just didn't want the children rummaging through the fridge at all hours. Even in her young age, Donna empathized with the story. Once, her mother had threatened to put a lock on the fridge when Donna and her girlfriends were up during the night devouring handfuls of cold cuts.

"Those are expensive," her mother had scorned. "If you're going to eat them, at least put them on bread."

Still, they were teenage girls and they had been ravenous. They ate the cold cuts in desperation and washed it all down with about a gallon of orange juice. Then, the sugar rush would carry them into whispering until dawn.

Joshua's story was different, though.

The parents' room he described was very dark. The walls were bare and the comforter on their bed was "unloving," he said, and covered in cat hair. In the corner of the room, there were shelves of boxed and canned foods — tunas, crackers, packages of dried fruit and jarred tomatoes. The little boy in the story sometimes stood at the doorway salivating, knowing his parents might be snacking inside the room. He didn't bother to try to enter much because the door was usually locked. And when he did enter, he'd curl up in a tiny ball between his parents and ask for a snack. His parents would cuddle him back but say something along the lines of, "You know when it is and when it is not time to eat."

In "Hunger," the efforts of the little boy's parents to keep their children from food became so neurotic that they began to use a tiny timer in the kitchen. When the light turned green, the children were allowed to eat. When the timer was dark, they were not allowed to eat.

The little boy was on the free lunch program at school but complained that every meal was a cheese sandwich and a glass of 1% milk. "Not even 2%," he wrote. "Not even 2."

In response, his mother wrote a letter to the kids, "When I read 'Hunger,' I wanted to die."

Now, Donna knew what hunger was.

Then, at the very bottom of the box, wrapped in another deliciously buttery, soft, small, turquoise scarf, there was a typewritten note. It appeared it had never been opened. Donna suspected it had, but that it had been handled with such care it was as if no one had ever touched it but her.

The note was titled "My Fantasy."

It was a detailed portrayal of a woman going into a horse stable and shooting herself in the face. It talked about the emotion leading up to the decision, the moments of discontent and uncertainty. She described placing her finger on the trigger again and again, dragging on for hours, wondering if it was the right decision.

In the end, the woman pulls the trigger and blood splatters across a delicate but strong white horse. The fantasy ends by saying, "I had that horse since I was a baby."

Donna sat and considered everything in the "Mom" box for a long while. It seemed Joshua had taken his mother's fantasy of shooting herself in the horse stable and made it come to life. She couldn't be sure whether he did this to lie or if he did it to cope. Maybe he had to stage her death to move on. Maybe he needed to live through such a gruesome suicide to leave her in his past.

In any case, a white horse splattered with blood did exist. That he had not lied about. But the white horse, Donna now knew, existed in a dream world. A dream world contained in a crisp, creamy envelope in a box in an attic. In a box in her grandmother's attic.

Now, in addition to needing to know how to bring Joshua down, Donna needed to know what had brought Joshua to her grandmother in the first place. She had the tools to make Joshua's life a living hell. But the big question overarching everything was: Why?

Why would he cling to a woman who was dying? Did he need a maternal figure in his life, or did he want to be a paternal figure to someone else? It seemed as though Joshua wanted to be both at once: a child and a parent.

There was something about this that seemed confusing to Donna. Maybe he needed to provide safety for someone in order to feel safe himself. Then maybe when Rudy passed away, he had really lost it. He had lost the person who played both roles and returned to the memory of his mother. He needed to symbolically kill his mother to move on.

Just as Donna put down the "Mom" package, she heard Joshua arrive downstairs. He put down his keys on the counter calmly and seemed to wade in the room like water. He called up to her simply, just saying "Hi, Donna."

CHAPTER TWENTY-FOUR: JUST SAYING HI

"Hi," was all she could manage to say, but it came after a long silence. She didn't feel caught out. It was her house after all. She had a right to be there whenever she wanted, no matter who was home or what lock was on the door or even what door was on the fucking frame.

"What did you find?" he asked.

"Not a lot," said Donna. She swallowed a little bit. Part of her was hiding her findings because she wanted to present them to her mother first, so they could strategize. The other part of her was hiding her new knowledge because she knew it could be triggering information for Joshua, which Ricky warned against. If he got too angry and joined her in the attic, it would be impossible for her to escape. She didn't know what he was capable of, and for all she knew he could push her down from the ceiling into the hardwood floor.

"I don't have a lot of stuff," Joshua said. "I didn't lie about that."

"Well, you skirted around the truth a bit," said Donna. "You have a lot more than you let on."

"Okay," said Joshua. She heard him set down a dish. It sounded like he was about to microwave a meal.

"What are you making?" Donna asked.

"A Lean Cuisine," he said. "Do you want one?"

Donna bit her lip. His intertwining of casual conversation with overarching trauma frustrated and scared the hell out of her. Still, she responded casually, too.

"I'm not hungry," she said. "But thanks."

She covered the "Mom" package with her sweatshirt and began to make her way down the creaky ladder. When she got to the bottom, she faced him.

"Thank you for killing the snake," she said.

"How's your leg?"

"It's fine."

"You have bad luck with that leg," Joshua said.

"And roommates," she said.

She and Joshua stared at each other for a while. For a second, it felt like they were friends again. Like they could laugh all this off and just move on. But Donna shook off the feeling. She knew it was all a part of his manipulation.

"You're in my way," said Joshua. "You've always been in my way, from the moment I first saw you. I watched you move in," he said. "The first time you pulled up to the house, I saw you go into the backyard and check it out. You knew right away something was off about the garden."

"Why did you move all the plants up to the front of the house?" she asked.

"Because I didn't want to look at it. I couldn't keep up with it. Rudy took care of the plants until the bitter end. No point in pretending I could care for them, too."

Donna rolled her eyes and huffed aggressively. "I can't believe you knew my grandmother."

"Yeah, I did," he spat sharply. "Better than you."

"Did you think she would leave you the house?"

"No," he said. "But it doesn't matter. You people were so sloppy with the will and the paperwork and the organization." He smiled. "I had no problem calling this place my own."

Donna wanted him to think he won.

"You're right," she said. "I was really dumb." She meant that part. "I didn't know what I was getting into. I just came out here because I thought it would be glamorous, I thought I would find myself, I don't know what I thought."

"Did any of that happen for you?" he asked.

"A little bit, actually," Donna said. "You've shown me how to allow myself to be sad. How to hole up in my room and really take care of myself when I need it. You've taught me a healthy way to cry. Deep, hard, belly cries that really get it all out. You've taught me it's okay to be in the darkness for a second." She took a breath. "Plus, the views around here are stellar."

"Excellent," he said. "Then you got what you needed. In a way."

The microwave was beeping. His Lean Cuisine was done. He pulled it out and set it on the counter. They stood in stillness and awkwardness for a while before he finally said, "It has to rest for five minutes."

"I always skip that part," said Donna.

"You shouldn't," said Joshua. "It's when the top gets crispy. It's when it fully bakes."

"Okay," she said. "Next time."

They were quiet for the entire five minutes. Donna was preoccupied staring at the plastic on top of the Lean Cuisine. She liked the way the bubbles of steam looked rising to the surface then popping slightly. It was a chicken parmesan with noodles and smelled great. She wondered what Ina Garten thought of Lean Cuisines. Surely she ate one every now and then.

"Look, Donna," said Joshua. "At the end of it, you remind me a lot of her. And that's what makes me like you."

"You . . . like me?" she asked. As if she cared. But she did. Ugh.

"I really like you," he said. "I would have killed you if I didn't."

What he said was scary, but Donna knew it wasn't true. Joshua never would have killed her, no matter how he felt. He was a different kind of evil. His evil was more subtle.

"You know I can't stay here," Donna said.

"I know," Joshua said.

"It just might take a while," she said.

"That's okay," said Joshua. "It's fine."

He uncovered his Lean Cuisine and took it to the sofa where he leaned back and propped up his feet. "Want to watch *Barefoot Contessa*?" he asked.

Donna was suddenly furious. She couldn't believe how easily the roles reversed. Now, it felt like she was visiting his space. And part of what he said was true — he had been close with her grandmother, apparently. He had known her, he had cared for her. If she never saw his malicious side, what did it even matter? He gave her companionship during her final days. Donna wondered why Rudy didn't put him in the will. Maybe it was because she was trying to preserve something — some sense of family, she felt she had lost her whole life.

"I should go, actually," she said.

Donna remembered her boyfriend back in Chicago, and how they stood in the cold for a moment when they broke up knowing things were over. There was a lingering, a last attempt to stay together. If something bold enough had happened in that moment, Donna wondered if they would have stayed together. Donna really didn't ask for much from people. It took very little to get her attention and hold it. Most importantly, she wanted to be excited and feel cared for.

Unfortunately for her, those two things rarely go together. Oftentimes, the most exciting people were the ones that harmed her. The people who nurtured her sometimes bored her to tears. She hoped in her life she could find somewhere in the middle.

But for now, looking at Joshua wrapped in a blanket on the sofa, eating a Lean Cuisine and starting up the television show, Donna believed that was what her grandmother had seen. For a second, she even found herself dreading the last time she would see him. One day, she would see him for the last time, and that would be it. She wasn't sure if she would know when that time was or if their relationship would just taper away. But she did know, for some sick, mysterious reason, that she would miss it.

CHAPTER TWENTY-FIVE: A WORK OF ART

Donna and Addie sat in the motel and debated what to do next. Addie was still bloodthirsty, but Donna wanted to soften a bit after learning of Joshua's childhood abuse. Then she reminded herself of the agony he had put her through — the arrest, the door change, the utter disrespect.

The room felt tense. Rising frustrations with Joshua were pitting the mother and daughter against one another. Neither knew what the right move would be, and it was clear Addie was building resentments. She was so deep in thought, the ash tip of her cigarette had begun to bend like a lazily moving caterpillar. Donna had been given a brand-new opportunity and, to both of their frustration, it had all gone wrong.

"What do you think should happen?" Donna asked.

"I think we should shoot him in the head," her mother said viciously. "But I know we're not going to do that. Can't we find a way to chase him out?"

"I don't know if 'chasing him out' is the right thing either, at this point," Donna said. "Because after all this, why would I even still want that house?"

"Because it's a free house," Addie snapped back in frustration. "You don't know how lucky you are. I'd give anything for it."

"I know," Donna said. "You keep talking about how I'm lucky and how I should be grateful, but it makes you sound loathing of your own life." She groaned. "It's annoying."

"I had to work for everything I got," Addie said. "A free house was never just passed on to me, okay?"

"Ugh — that's the most basic answer!" Donna said, her temper rising. "You always act like I don't work for anything. I've had at least a part-time job every day since I was sixteen years old."

"I know that," Addie said. "You're a hard worker and I admire that. But . . ." she said, seeming to tread carefully, "you've continuously lacked some sort of, I don't know."

"*What?*" Donna pried.

"Ambition." Addie exhaled. "You've tended to lack some ambition."

"Ambition?" Donna asked. "What are you even talking about?"

"My side of the family, Donna, we've always had our eye on the target. That's why we give you such a hard time, okay? Nobody knows what you want. You're sort of, well, lackadaisical, honestly, maybe something you inherited from your father."

Donna prickled. Since her father died, all her less-than-lovable traits seemed to be blamed on him. "I'm not lackadaisical," she said. "You're putting this on me because you're jealous."

"I am jealous," Addie agreed, obviously trying to lower the heat on the situation. "Look — I'm happy, honey. I'm happy for the life I've had, even with all its downfalls. And I'm happy I have you. But even though I'm your mom, you can't forget I'm a person, too. Sometimes I feel like you do. Sometimes I want to, you know, go to the oceanside and the cliffs, too. And feel alone and beautiful and like nature is just right fucking there. That melancholy aloneness you get to feel sometimes, lest we forget, is a privilege."

"A privilege to be sad. Okay."

"I want to be sad on the side of a cliff in California!" Addie said. "And fantasize about jumping off, even!"

Donna's eyes widened. She had never heard her mother reference suicide so casually. "Not because I don't like my life," Addie added. "Just the possibilities, Donna, the could-have-beens."

Donna didn't know what to say. She curled her hands around the soles of her feet and pulled herself in even tighter.

"Once you have a family, everything gets prescribed to you," Addie went on. "So even in my brief depressive whims, I have to think about everybody else. So, what I'm saying is, if I were Joshua's mom and I wrote a detailed fantasy about how to off myself and wrapped it in a cute tiny little scarf, I'd keep it far away from you. Because that's all it is. It's a fantasy. It's when you scrape a suicide note on a half-used yellow pad that you really have a problem."

"I think if you wrap it in a cute little scarf you still have a problem. Clearly."

Addie sighed. "I guess what I'm saying is, I don't think Joshua's mom really wants to kill herself at all. I think it's all a show. And I think that's what drives Joshua crazy."

Donna knew Addie was right. And she was hurt her own mother had called her lackadaisical. To set the record straight, she knew she could either gain control of the turmoil in her life or she would continue to disappoint her mom. But her mom was wrong that she didn't have her eye on a target. Donna did have a target. Joshua. She wanted to upset him in the same way his mother had — by making everything all a show.

The suffering Joshua's mother had experienced and caused had been largely performative, artistic even. When pondering the ways to get Joshua to the core, Donna felt like she had to level up on the performativity somehow. She thought of all the things in life that were performative — plays at the theatre, cinema, museums. When she thought about museums her stomach filled with butterflies. In her fantasies about Cole, she would bring him back home for a holiday and show him the Art Institute of Chicago. Donna and her mother had spent so much time there when she was a girl. She loved wearing the big headphones and wandering the rooms, listening to stories about the artists' lives and feeling deep and angsty. She wondered if she could recreate some of those feelings in Joshua — the despair art could cause in her early adolescence.

One painting in particular came to mind, the "Farm Near Duivendrecht." She remembered it vividly because the scene had struck her as both tranquil and sad. It depicted a farmhouse in Holland at what seems to be sunrise — stark, leafless trees surround a lonely farm that's reflected in a small pond. As a child, she always thought the painting was sort of dreadful and sad. It looked cold, just like Chicago. For whatever reason, she related to it, and wondered if Joshua would, too.

The cold farm wasn't unlike the farm described in the fantasy, but it needed a bit of finessing. Although the idea was elaborate, Donna wondered if she could transform the contents of Joshua's mother's fantasy into some kind of artwork. In a strange way, she felt this could both honor Joshua's experience and alter it. She wanted him to feel unsettled, haunted, in the most visceral way possible without violence or threats.

She brought the idea up to Addie, who immediately knew the painting Donna was referencing. "I always found that one to be odd, too," she agreed, "for whatever reason."

"Do you think it's a good idea?" Donna asked. "To deliver some kind of artwork?"

"It's weird," said Addie slowly. "But it might be weird enough to work."

The two discussed what the artwork would even look like. The missing piece to the "Farm Near Duivendrecht" was, of course, the horse. But tonally it was nearly spot on. They considered a big painted canvas with a splattered white horse, or a more conceptual piece that included some of the keywords from her letter.

As they thought about it, their creativity took a more gruesome route. They thought of a collage of suicide portraits, things that would remind him of what his mother must have felt as she sat down to write the note. Their ideas seemed more and more cruel. What Donna pictured didn't seem so bad, but when she said her ideas aloud, she would follow them up with throwaways like, "That's so fucked up."

In the end, they agreed subtle was best. "It will mean more to him, I think, if what makes it disturbing is the context," Addie's mom said in a way that only a non-artist could talk about art. "Like a coded message. Something that might seem innocuous at first sight."

Donna thought of what this could be. She had an idea.

A large, grim horse stable. She could picture the lighting, even. A hopeless dark room with a tiny sliver of light creeping in. She pictured the hay in the background of the piece, half-eaten. Shadows of leafless trees rising in. She had no idea how to begin such a painting — she certainly wouldn't be able to paint it herself. It was the realistic style of only one person she knew — Cole.

CHAPTER TWENTY-SIX: THE STABLE

When she called Cole, he was surprised. He said he was beginning to worry she wouldn't call again. "I even considered moving," he said. "Every little thing was reminding me of you."

"How's your arm?" she asked.

"It's healing," he said.

"I'm sorry," said Donna. "I'm sorry about everything. I'm sorry I didn't move quickly enough for you, I'm sorry about all the faith I put in Joshua, I'm sorry you were hurt." She inhaled sharply. "I care about you so much."

"You have a funny way of showing it," he said. "But I care about you, too. Immensely."

"I know," she said. She did know. She had been too hard on Cole from the beginning. She didn't listen to him, didn't give their budding romance a fair shot. "I've come up with a plan for a final gesture," she said. "But I need to pick your brain."

"A final gesture," he said hopefully. "You're moving out?"

"We're hoping actually to drive him out," she said. "If that doesn't work, we sell."

"Donna . . ." he hesitated. "I don't know."

"Please, Cole," Donna begged. "You said you needed the start of a plan and that's what I have."

Cole laughed. "You piece of shit." But then rather than saying goodbye, he said, "Yes. Okay. I'll help."

They had a lot of catching up to do. Donna explained the contents of the mom box, the stable and the story. "I want to make some kind of artwork," she said, "some design to evoke all this feeling. I want to shake him up."

"You have to understand that this man stabbed me in the arm for simply picking up some trash," Cole said. "You can't blame me for being a little cautious."

"Well, that's why I wanted to abstract the situation," Donna said. She paced the motel room, still in her sleeping gown. Addie sat interested on the edge of the bed.

"If it's just an artwork, I mean what's he gonna do — cry?"

"Or hopefully have a full-blown nervous breakdown," Donna said.

For a second, Cole sounded unsure. It seemed like he was itching to get off the phone as soon as possible. But then, he reached a conclusion. "A painting, huh? Is there any way I could just make it a little more me?" he asked.

"Yeah," Donna said. She gave her mother a big smile. "You can make it as you as you want."

* * *

When Cole arrived, Addie nodded to Donna in approval. It was clear she thought he was super cute.

"Adelina," she said, shaking his hand energetically.

"I'm Cole," he said, smiling, and rolled out a drawing pad onto the bed. With Donna's guidance, he made a few sketches. She felt like an art director — and he was the artist. What Donna liked so much about Cole's art in the first place was the detail. She loved how he could manage such a wide range of feelings without taking too many artistic liberties. He had a knack for portraying the scene as is but with a deep emotional core. After some brainstorming, they thought a painting of a stable could be effective. In

Donna's wildest dreams, it would be as realistic as possible, but Cole talked her down and said that could take years. They compromised on something that could just take a few days of dedicated work: a simple white horse in the stable of a gray, dying field.

"Are you sure you want to do this?" Donna asked. "I don't want to introduce more drama."

"I'm happy to help in the revenge scenario," Cole said. "I mean, this dude did fuck up my arm," he laughed. "And my relationship. And my brain."

Donna gave her mother, who was sitting nearby, a thumbs up. "I think we hired the right person," she said.

Cole got to work. In the meantime, Donna and Addie continued to live in the motel nearby. Donna visited the house frequently and placed her possessions into boxes. She wanted to create the illusion that Joshua had, in fact, won. He was mostly reasonable during her visits. They didn't speak much, but for the next two weeks she went in and out of the house and they coexisted peacefully. Donna began to realize how little stuff she had. After finding Joshua's secret stash in the attic, she maybe had fewer belongings than he did.

What was interesting about the encounters was that Joshua was helpful. He helped her consolidate her books into well-packed boxes. He helped rearrange the heavy items and organize what should stay and what should go. During all the visits, Donna's interior was screaming, "It's all mine, you fucking asshole!" But to him, Rudy's belongings were his and the remainder of the items were Donna's.

Joshua's room did not look nearly as showy as it had the evening of his fortieth birthday party. The air had grown stale again. The party items were still there, but with far less panache. Everything was still staged but sulky, especially the rug and the lighting. By now, a couple of the bulbs were out. The empty snake tank looked pathetic.

Donna offered to help him clean the terrarium out, and he agreed. "But I don't want to move the whole tank out," he said. "I'm considering buying another pet."

Donna wanted to hurl objects at him and tell him he was an animal abuser. That snake had been improperly cared for. It had lived in a dark closet for most of its stay in California and it had been a miserable animal that wanted to eat people as soon as they blinked an eye. Donna felt sorry for the snake — the way his life ended was ungraceful — he had been a wild animal trapped in domesticity, living against his nature.

Donna called Cole a few times to see how the project was going. She didn't want to drive him mad, but equally, he was very tight-lipped about it, which made Donna concerned. She wanted it to be good, and she wanted its nuance to disturb Joshua more than anything else.

Back at the motel, Donna tried to help her mom work through a plan to become less static and miserable. One benefit of this tumultuous period was that it gave everyone a chance to have some kind of rebirth. The trauma of it all forced everyone to reflect and try to get their shit together. Donna wasn't sure what her future had in store, but she had a lot of life left to live. Her mother had plenty of life, too, but less so. Her happiness took priority.

At any mention of dating and looking for a partner, though, Addie completely withdrew. She wanted to be alone, and Donna didn't blame her. Her father had been good to her but terrible to her mother. He hadn't been violent, didn't even yell, and was helpful around the house. But what had been terrible about him was that he had just pretended as though her mother didn't exist. Donna observed this from an early age. He would walk into a room and greet everyone in the room except his partner. When leaving, he would say goodbye to everyone but her. They never slept in the same room, never watched television together, never went out together. For a long while, Donna witnessed her mom making a big effort for him. But after a period of no effort returned, she just gave up. She still looked nice and did fun activities and told funny stories, but she just never did it for him anymore. She did it for Donna. She wanted to look after her daughter and make her feel at home.

Donna didn't know much about Cole's family, but they seemed relatively stable. Many of the realities that surfaced from Joshua's past deeply disturbed Cole. He couldn't fathom going through some of those tribulations and concluded that "Hunger" was a story told from experience. It was like Joshua wrote it as a demand for attention, but then when his teacher threw a safety line into the water, he didn't take it.

Joshua was like that. All he wanted was to alert people around him that he needed to be saved — but when the time came for safety, he rejected it.

Donna wondered what the painting was going to be like. She was certain it would be beautiful, which would maybe make it a waste. It was being used for more than just revenge though. It was a tool to deepen an ongoing problem. Some part of her hoped that in addition to breaking Joshua down, it would give him some resources to also build him back up. She didn't want him to live in squalor forever. She wanted him to heal so he could stop fucking other people's lives up.

While she waited for the painting to be finished, she reached out to Joshua's biological sister. Melanie spoke in a distinct, scratchy-sounding voice and owned a lot of birds. Right after Donna got her on the phone, she could hear Melanie cracking ice out of the tray and pouring herself a beverage, undoubtedly alcohol. Then in the background throughout their conversation, she heard frantic squeaks and squawks and cages ratting and the flapping of wings. Even being on the other side of the phone gave her anxiety.

Melanie, in addition to owning birds, was one of those people who almost exclusively talked about owning birds. Everything came back to the birds. How they helped her recover from trauma, how she used them as a tool for survival and how they were just "too damn pretty to pass up."

She said she wanted to get one bird, but after warming up with that bird in the home, she needed more and more. It was like an addiction, she called it, "comparable to people with tattoos, you know, you get one and then you want a bunch of tats right in a row. That's me and birds, that's me.

And. Birds." Donna didn't know what to say. "Do you have any tattoos?" Melanie asked.

"I don't," Donna said. "I was calling to ask you a little bit about Joshua, or, sorry, Donovan."

"Joshua," she laughed. "Is that the name he's going by nowadays?"

"Why are you laughing?" Donna asked.

"Because he's fucked up," Melanie said. "Nothing I hear about him could surprise me. You know it's a big problem, the squatter stuff. It's out of control because those squatters have the same rights that normal tenants have."

"I know," said Donna. "I did a lot of research on it."

"In California it's especially bad," Melanie went on. "The laws were put in place to protect tenants from their landlords, but what ends up happening is actually an abuse of landlords and property owners." She coughed and a bird chirped close to the phone, maybe propped up on her shoulder. "Sorry," she said. "That's tequila. What was I saying? Oh. In California it's bad because there are so many abandoned homes, or homes that go through renovations and this and that. The squatters just take the opportunity right when they get the chance. Joshua popped into a few places over the years, including my brother's place. Shit gets nasty. No none can get rid of him."

"Have you . . . gotten rid of him?" Donna said.

"I send him a text every now and again," Melanie said. "I'm not a monster. But do I try to avoid him at all costs? Yes." She clinked her glass in a way that seemed finite. Was it possible her drink was already gone?

"Melanie, can I ask you something? I just want to find out some more information about your family because of what I'm going through with Donovan. When was the last time you heard from your mother?"

"Oh, man," she trailed off. "We were teenagers."

"So she wasn't the best mom," Donna presumed.

"No, quite the opposite. She was a great mom for so long, so when she suddenly wasn't anymore, it just made it even more painful."

"Do you know where she is?" Donna asked.

"I think she's in Nevada," Melanie said. "Last I heard, Donovan's the only one of us that still talks to her."

Donna wasn't sure if she should share this, but she felt a strange kinship with Melanie, like the kinship she felt initially with Joshua.

"He told me she killed herself earlier this year. That she went into a horse stable and shot her brains out. Sorry to be graphic."

"Oh. No. I woulda heard about that," Melanie said. She sounded sure.

Donna was quiet for a second, trying to process the new information she was getting. "Is it possible Donovan visited her this year?"

"It's definitely possible," Melanie said. "They do holidays together and all that. But Ricky and I, that's my other brother, we just don't put up with the bullshit anymore. I got a life and a family of my own. Got my birds, anyway. They're all I need."

"When you say Donovan is fucked up, what exactly do you mean?"

"I mean, he just doesn't feel like the rest of us. Do you understand? I mean, you're human, I'm human. Donovan may as well be an alien. He's a soul sucker. He just strips people of their resources, their time, their worth."

"He went to prison the first time for a threat," Donna said. "Do you think it's talk or — is he really dangerous?"

"Oh, yeah. Oh, yeah," Melanie said. "Once, when we were kids, he held a dagger to my throat so I'd let him stay in my room."

"He didn't want to be alone?"

"Yeah, or he just wanted what was mine," Melanie said. Now, Donna heard ice clinking again. She thought Melanie was pouring herself another drink and didn't blame her. She could use a drink, too.

"One more thing," Donna said. "And I'm sorry if I'm overstepping, it's just, I'm trying to put together some pieces."

"What is this for again?"

"I just know Donovan and have been worried about him."

"Don't be too worried," Melanie said flippantly. "He'll never worry back."

This stung a bit, but Donna wasn't totally sure why, so she continued. "Did your parents used to, um, hide food in their room?"

She heard breathing but didn't get a response.

"Melanie?" Melanie still just breathed and clinked her glass and didn't answer. Donna tried one more time. "Hello?"

"Hi, I'm here. Hi," Melanie said. "There's a lot I've had to, you know, block out. I don't know if you have stuff like that, but I do. A lot of that stuff, listen, I don't even remember. I've had to train myself to forget. It's taken a lot of work and I don't want to talk about it."

"I understand," Donna said. And she did. "I'll let you go."

After a pause, Melanie said, "They did. They did hide food in their room."

"Okay," said Donna. "Okay. Thank you."

"Uh-huh," Melanie said. "Bye now."

Donna hoped their phone conversation didn't open too many wounds for Melanie. Everything that was going awry with Joshua had nothing to do with her, or Ricky, or the house even. It seemed like the root causes of pain were Joshua and their parents.

To Donna, the sick thing was that it sounded as if Joshua kept a relationship with his mother. One that he kept watering and refused to let go of. And she thought he tried to let go of her. He tried to get away, move from LA, and psychologically kill her even. He put her in a stable where she held a gun to her head in front of her favorite childhood horse and just let her pull the trigger. He went through the stages of grief. He staged a memorial for someone who was very much alive.

* * *

In the bustle of new information, Donna wanted to call Aunt Sheeba and give a full report. Sheeba answered and sounded quieter than usual — her signature bite was lacking. And though she was excited to hear the case was going so well, she admitted she wasn't feeling well. This saddened Donna, who hoped she could get in on the action. "I'm just tired," Aunt Sheeba insisted. "Don't let my state spoil your fun." Donna let out a cough-laugh at this. Though everything was unpredictable and scary, she did have to admit it was a little fun. "Soon you'll have enough to go back to your lawyer, Roberta," she said. Donna froze. "That is the plan, isn't it?" Because of the risky business, Donna had spared Sheeba the details about Addie and Cole and the plan of action. The detective work had been thrilling, but Donna didn't want her to worry too much.

"Soon enough," was all Donna said, and let Aunt Sheeba go get some rest.

After hanging up, Donna called the salon owner to see if she could take a few days of vacation — coincidentally, the other receptionist was looking for more hours, so the timing worked out nicely. When their conversation was finished, the owner said Lydia was nearby and wanted to say hello. Donna was relieved. The salon had been so busy lately, she hadn't been able to share any of her news.

"I've been thinking about you," Lydia said. Donna heard her jewelry — likely a pair of big, colorful earrings — tinkling into the receiver. "We've barely talked since the party."

"I have a lot to tell you," said Donna. "Is everything okay with you?"

Lydia quieted her voice. "Happy six months, by the way," she said. "You're getting a raise."

Donna exhaled, thrilled. In all the action, at least she knew she was doing something right.

The raise in combination with an approved vacation gave Donna fresh momentum. She kept her eye on the target — Joshua. If she could tackle the Joshua problem, her situation would be on a better course. She may even be able to resume her relationship with Cole before too long.

After a few days of staying in the motel, on an unusually cool morning in early summer, the painting was complete. At the time, Donna was back at Rudy's, packing up the last of her things. She told Cole to drive to meet Addie at the hotel immediately.

* * *

The group wanted the unveiling of the painting to feel just right. They opened a crisp bottle of white to commemorate it, and Donna cleared a space in the room so the background would be as neutral as possible.

Shyly, Cole pulled back the corners of the painting. Donna and her mother both gasped.

At first look, the piece was delightful. The canvas was painted a creamy white, just as Donna had envisioned. The background was as thick as nail lacquer and smooth. Donna couldn't identify a single brush stroke. Overlaying the cream background, a finessed brown of a stable. The detail-work was incredible — Donna couldn't believe Cole had done it in just a few days. It made her love Cole even more. In the center of the stable, grazing peacefully, was a Camarillo white horse. The painting looked almost like a black-and-white vintage photograph. It was stunning — it shattered Donna.

The title of the painting, as Cole called it, was "The Fantasy."

They sat and sipped their wine and stared at it for a long while. "I'm feeling so much," Donna said. "I barely know what to say."

"I would put it in my own house," Addie kept saying. "I'm serious!"

"It's just what I wanted, Cole," Donna said. "Nice work." She wanted to jump his bones, but her mom was there. So Cole crashed on the pallet, and Donna and Addie climbed into bed. In the morning, the three of them would get up early and drive to Grandmother Rudy's house.

Donna slept poorly, waking up at different points and listening to her mom and Cole breathing. The breath as a soundtrack to the painting in half-darkness was unsettling. She had disjointed dreams about the horse and the blood and the envelope and the attic. In the morning, Cole said he had a dream that Joshua's mother shot herself in front of the painting, and the blood went all over the creamy white background, the background he spent hours perfecting.

He said he wondered how the horse would have felt.

CHAPTER TWENTY-SEVEN: GRANDMA'S HOUSE

It was a beautiful day. Donna and the others had woken up feeling refreshed, despite the anxiety-ridden night. She felt an oncoming sense of closure, something they had craved for so many days. She wasn't sure how the closure would play out, but the three expressed certainty that it would launch a new chapter of life — one that didn't revolve around Joshua Flowers or Grandmother Rudy's house.

They took Cole's truck, since the painting would fit in the back. Donna and Addie crowded into the front, Donna in the middle and her mother in shotgun. On the way, nobody spoke much, and they listened to music on the radio. Strangely, Donna didn't know any of the songs. She always knew all the words to all the mainstream radio and loved to sing along. She wasn't sure when that had ended, but she realized during that ride she had been removed from pop culture since her relocation to California. The salon played a pretentious sort of jazzy hip hop that made Donna feel like she was high on MDMA whenever she turned it on. But in the car that morning, Donna couldn't remember the last time she went dancing or played music in the shower or even just rode along and sang to the radio. Lately, she had been driving in silence.

She paid special attention to the leaves on the side of the road that day. As they all piled up in their springy greens and flowers, Donna felt that sense of rebirth she had craved when she first moved to California.

The three decided the best person to present the painting would be Donna. They expected Joshua's reaction to be a slow, simmering burn, but Addie had brought the gun just in case. Donna thought that was a bit dramatic — especially after everything that happened with the snake, surely no one was going to get shot.

It occurred to Donna that Joshua might be appreciative of the painting. Maybe he would see it and feel understood, or like someone had tried to know him more deeply. Addie seemed to think that was missing the point. She wanted to destroy his very existence with this thing. Otherwise, she would have wasted an inordinate amount of time in a completely different state in a dingy hotel room living bitterly and vicariously through her daughter's life.

When they arrived at the house, Donna suddenly saw what it really was for the first time. She saw what it had become. In under a year, the house had devolved into less of a grandmother's house and into more of a crack house. The IKEA doors looked terrible. The lawn was overgrown, and the porch was unswept. In the early morning light, the porch light should have still been on timer, but it was out. The eastern sun hit the house in a way that made the blue paint seem a moldy green. The porch was covered in dust. The chair and table were tilted — everything looked out of place.

The garden boxes that Rudy had tended to so kindly in the backyard now looked like children's sandboxes that had been overgrown with weeds. Gnats and other bugs circulated. Through the windows, blinds hung ajar, and curtains were tossed to the perimeters carelessly. There were fingerprints visible on the inside of the windows, as if someone had carelessly tried to clean with a paper towel and water and gave up.

A pile of junk mail seeped out of the mailbox. It reminded Donna of a drug addict — someone who took too many too fast and just totally unraveled. She blinked back tears thinking of the hope she had put into this place and how jealous her mother was of it. When they first arrived, it was spic and span. She thought she may grow to find love in that house, to potentially marry someone and raise children there, or at least get old there gracefully by herself. She looked over at Cole and felt her heart break. Surely she wouldn't stay in California much longer. She didn't know what could be in store for them. Too much was at stake. The lovers had become burnt out and frustrated too early on, and she was afraid it was time to move along.

His thin face was so handsome. In the reflection of his dark, muddy, green eyes, Donna saw the dark reflection of the trees in the front yard. That was the one thing about the house that still looked beautiful — the trees. And looking back at the trees, it seemed like they reflected Cole's eyes, too. Donna couldn't decide which was greener.

She thought of Cole's artwork. Even if he had grown tired and sore about Donna, he had made the painting to appease her. That made her feel loved, even if the situation was bizarre. She felt strange, and empty almost.

"Are you ready?" Cole asked, and Donna realized they had been sitting in front of the house for a long while. She'd recently found that, increasingly, her mind drifted like that. Maybe it was her growing sense of disarray that made her just shut the world out sometimes. Her mother had also spaced out. The apple and the tree and however it goes, Donna and Addie were startlingly similar.

Cole and Donna locked eyes and had a shared moment of appreciation. She was happy to know him. She was happy for the rush and the suddenness of their love. She was happy for what he had taught her, and the time they had spent together.

She didn't know what was next for them — she was worried he no longer saw love in her like he had before. Maybe there was friendship and understanding, but that was it. She let it soak in that it might be the last day she would get to see him, at least for a while. But amidst everything, that felt right. She didn't know what more she could possibly give him. At a certain point, she wasn't giving — she was only taking. But she hoped that no matter what, it wasn't the end of their story.

"I want to say something first," Donna's mother said, "about the painting."

Packed in the car, they weren't able to crane their necks to look at her.

"Even if this is a revenge painting, or whatever it is," she began, "it is lovely, Cole. In a way, the painting will also honor this house. It will honor the strangeness of it. The strangeness of Joshua, and the strangeness of Rudy who — honestly — was a bit of a weird bird. She would have liked the painting, too. I'm sure of it. So, whatever happens in a few minutes' time, I just want us to remember that. That we are doing the house some good." Then she laughed a little bit. "I mean, if you saw this at Pier 1 without context or something, it would make a great display."

"Thank you," Cole said.

"Even for normal people!" Addie added.

"Thank you," Cole said again.

Donna's heart felt full of rocks. She was so afraid of what was to come, but she had support and she had it under control. It was time to say goodbye to Joshua, goodbye to Rudy, goodbye to California, for a long while. Maybe even forever.

"Can you take a picture of me?" she asked Cole.

"It would be my honor," he said, and took the pink Polaroid in his hands. Donna walked to the center of the garden boxes, in front of the overgrown crack-looking house, and forced the biggest smile she could muster. She wanted to look back on it and think she was pretty. She felt pretty. She felt pretty and deranged like she had thrown a bomb into her life. For whatever reason, she settled into all that. She liked knowing Cole was behind the camera and that her mother was nearby. She would always remember that.

CHAPTER TWENTY-EIGHT: HEADSPACE

They didn't need to walk into the house to see Joshua. He came outside to greet them. "Did you forget something?" he asked Donna. He seemed sincere.

"No, I didn't," Donna said slowly. "Can we come in for a few minutes? I have something to give to you."

Joshua's eyes scanned across the group. He looked suspicious. Donna was sure that even Joshua could agree that everything on Earth had been upended in the last year, even if he was the cause of most of it. "Sure," he said. "I'd be happy to have you."

"We'll follow you in," Donna said. "Just give us a minute to grab our stuff."

"Okay," Joshua said. "I'll get a pot of coffee going."

Joshua turned gracefully. Donna looked at her mother and sucked air in through her teeth. Addie did the same back.

They eased their way up to the house and heard Joshua on the inside, grinding coffee beans. Joshua seemed more settled than ever before, playing the role of a proper host.

"Donna," he began, his back still turned to them. He was facing the coffee pot — his movements as elegant as ever. "I'm glad you came by the house. I have wanted to thank you but didn't know how." He poured the fresh grounds into the pot and began to run water from the sink into the large cup. "You must think I'm insane," he said. "I've had a rough year. Between Rudy's death and the death of my mom, it's just like — it's been like — all my guidance is gone. You know how I mean."

"I know," Donna said. "It's been tough for everyone. She was my grandmother after all."

Joshua looked harsh for a moment. His eyebrow furrowed just slightly. "You barely even spoke to her," he said. Then, "Never mind, that's not the point." He hit the power button on the coffee pot and waited for it to make a humming sound, ready to serve. "The reason I want to thank you is because you've been reasonable throughout. I haven't been perfect. Neither have you. But at the end of the day, I'm glad we met and I'm regretful that it had to end this way. But I think we can both agree I care for this place more out of the two of us and I feel more of a sense of home here," he said. "It's just I'm becoming something here. It wasn't expected, but I am. Thank you, seriously, for everything you did for me. Everything you taught me. I liked laughing with you, I liked watching TV with you, I liked drinking pink wine and eating meats and cheeses with you. We had our differences, but I will carry the fine memories with me always. I don't want you to forget the good."

Donna was not looking at Joshua. She was looking at her mother. Then, she looked to Cole, who was confidently staring at the large rectangular mass that was still covered with a tarp.

"I appreciate you saying thank you," Donna said. "Really, I do." She paused.

"And?" said Joshua.

"And what? That's it." Donna sounded harsher than she intended. She almost held her tongue but then couldn't help it. "Actually, you've made a big fucking mess of my life and of everything and while I appreciate the meat boards and you helping me move out and even the kind way you're making us all coffee at the moment, it's going to be really fucking hard to forget or come close to forgiving you for everything you have done to me."

"Donna—" Addie said, seemingly afraid of escalating the confrontation too soon. But Donna kept talking.

"I'm almost done. It's not all bad, but I need you to be aware of the damage you've caused me and how drastically you have altered my view of myself and my self-esteem. I am a different person from when I met you. And a lot of this new person is stronger and more careful and more cautious, but she's also got a drinking problem and she's angry all the time and she's just, like, bewildered, so yeah. There's that, too. So I do have stuff to thank you for, I do, but I have to add a big fuck you."

To everyone's surprise, Joshua said, "Okay." He kept his distance, but Donna felt like he was touching her shoulders. "It's okay. I'm glad you said it."

Donna laughed in a self-deprecating way.

"No, it's important to share how you feel. It's a part of the human experience," Joshua said. The coffee pot beeped. It was ready. Joshua poured each of the coffees by hand and placed them all on the side of the table. "Take a seat," he said. "We can talk."

They all followed instructions and sat down. Joshua started laughing.

"What's funny?" asked Donna's mom.

"I was thinking, the last time I was here with you two ladies, we had just shot my snake."

"That's true," said Addie. She sounded unamused and took a sip of her coffee.

They all sipped coffee and looked around the room. The elements that were like Rudy were dwindling away. There was barely a trace of her left.

Donna broke the silence first. "Want to know why we're here?" and gestured to the painting propped on the floor nearby. "I brought something for you," she continued, confidently. "A parting gift," she said. There was a strange silence. Joshua looked fulfilled, like it was solidified that Donna was giving up on the battle and the house would be his. "Would you like to see it?" she asked.

"Sure," said Joshua.

Donna's hands trembled as she got closer to the painting. She was overcome with fear, shaking and doubting if they should have put in the effort at all. In the best-case scenario, Joshua would be humiliated. In the worst-case scenario, consequences could become fatal. She assured herself that either situation would be worth it. After everything that had happened to her, after everything this horrible man put her through, she deserved to make him feel something. Whatever that something was, she didn't care. She just needed him to see the work they had conjured and created.

Donna pulled the tarp away from the picture.

"A painting," said Joshua, sounding surprised. "It's nice."

The three watched quietly because they knew Joshua hadn't internalized the painting yet. He got closer to it and knelt by it. His eyes moved quickly around every corner. "The work here is outstanding," he said. "It's beautiful, actually. I think this will really tie the room together."

"Thank you," said Donna. "I thought so, too."

They continued to watch Joshua as his eyes moved all around. Then, there was a slow dawning. "What is this painting called?" he asked, with just a tinge of fear in his voice.

"It's called 'The Fantasy'," Donna said. "Do you like it?"

Joshua took a step back and stumbled on one of the kitchen chairs. "That's a stable," he said in disbelief. "And that's . . ." he looked at the grazing horse in the center of the work. "I didn't see that at first, that's . . . my mother's, um, Rookie."

"It is," Donna said. "And one more thing." She reached into her jacket pocket and pulled out his mother's letter. "It was such a pretty little thing. We thought it would be perfect in a work of art, you know, to commemorate your mother's death."

"Donna," said Joshua.

"I read it, and I read the rest of the stuff in her box in the attic."

"Where is it?"

"I threw it away."

He looked at the envelope. "And that's all that's left?"

Donna hummed and nodded. "Yep."

"Can I have it back please?" Joshua asked. He was almost begging. "Please." He looked back to the painting. He couldn't take his eyes off it.

Then Joshua started to cry. It wasn't a pathetic kind of crying, like the tantrum he had thrown at Donna a few weeks ago. It was a real, repressed, overstimulated sort of crying, like the crying a child does into his mother's breast when he just can't take it anymore.

"Why did you tell me she died?" Donna asked.

"Because I wanted her to die," Joshua said. "Not in reality, but I wanted her to be dead to me."

"That day when you came home and I was in the attic," Donna began, "you didn't think I would find this?"

"There's a lot of stuff I black out," Joshua said. "Or maybe I wanted you to know, I don't know, subconsciously. I don't know why." His tears fell slowly down his face. Then, his face twisted up in the way it frequently did. His sorrow began to turn to frustration before their eyes. "Why did you do this?" he asked. "This took so much effort. Just to cause me pain. Why?"

"I wanted to get to you," said Donna. "Did I?"

"Yeah," said Joshua. "Congratulations. You got to me. Who did this?"

"I did," said Cole. "Where do you want me to hang it?"

"Oh yeah, you're the artist," Joshua said. He cocked his head at Cole, seemingly taken aback by his confidence, maybe having thought Cole would have backed down or showed some insecurity. After the way he treated Cole last time he saw him, he didn't think Cole could possibly want to test the waters. "Let me think about it for a second."

He went to the sink and splashed cold water on his face. The trio looked at one another in relief. They had gotten to him in a sweet spot. For a second, everything seemed satisfying. It was the ending they had hoped for.

Joshua ran the cold water over his eyes and tried to recompose himself. He finally lifted his head up and patted his face dry with a delicate kitchen towel Rudy had left behind. The towel was similar in pattern to one of Joshua's mother's scarves. It was one of those textiles only a woman would buy, a textile only a woman would keep clean and care for and keep for years. Joshua looked so in his element using it, as if the towel's very existence gave him just the comforting hug he needed.

"She has a lot of problems," he said. "My mother. I don't want you to think I faked her death for nothing."

"I don't," said Donna. "I get the idea she has a lot to work out, that she's still working out. Why did you still go and visit her?" she asked.

"I didn't," said Joshua. "I just went to her neighborhood and lingered around for a while. I wanted to be in the same place as she was. I was hoping to run into her, or ramp up the courage to say something, but I couldn't." Joshua walked toward Addie with a strange smile. "Do you remember after I shot the snake, you were worried that I didn't have my bath?" he asked.

"What?" Cole said.

"I was running a bath when they showed up. Then after I shot my own snake in the head and went to turn off the water, of all things, Donna's mother was worried that I wouldn't be able to take my bath." Joshua started to laugh a little bit. "I felt really cared for," he said. Perhaps it did mean a lot to him that someone cared whether he would take a bath or not, Donna thought. Not many other people in his life had cared for him in that way.

"I don't want anyone to go hungry or dirty or cold when they're around me," Donna's mother said. "Not even my worst enemies."

"Donna, am I your worst enemy?" he asked.

Donna wrinkled her brow. She didn't know what to say. She wanted to explode. She wanted to hang the painting in the center of the room and put a spotlight on it and go. She wanted to tie it up with chains and locks so he would never be able to take it down. She wanted him to face it every day.

"I think you are," she said.

"Cole?" he asked. "What about you? Am I your worst enemy, too?"

Cole kept a straight face and stared directly into Joshua's eyes. "I don't care much for you either way," he said.

"Then why'd you make me this painting?" Joshua smiled. His signature Halloween grin was back.

"I thought it suited you," said Cole, neutrally. "So, where do you want me to hang it?"

"Let's see . . ." said Joshua. "How about right here?"

Donna was surprised by his willingness to put the painting up. In a way, it annoyed her. She wasn't trying to give him a gift he liked, but rather to shake him up. She looked at Addie, who raised her eyebrows and shrugged discreetly. Donna felt the suspense of what could happen next. Her stomach hardened in anticipation.

Joshua pointed to a prominent wall right above the sofa. "I can get a toolbox for you." He went into the hall closet. From it, he pulled a big, black shiny toolbox and sorted meticulously through drill bits and screws.

"I got it," said Cole. "You can just relax."

Joshua stood close behind Cole and watched him pull the drill out and piece the two parts together. Once the drill was ready, Cole took off his shoes and stood on the couch and asked the group to help find the center point. Everyone had some slight disagreements — Joshua even offered to get out the tape measure to make sure it was perfect. No placement seemed good enough for Addie, who seemed to have lost sight of the agenda in order to get the painting up perfectly. But finally, the group agreed on where the middle was and got ready to hang the heavy canvas.

Cole drew two dots in place with a light pencil. Then, he held the painting up to where it would go. It really did suit the room well and make even Joshua's dreary decor come together. The tragedy of the painting was what made it the most beautiful. Even without any context, there was something raw about it. Piercing. And its size made it seem elegant and prestigious.

Cole spun the two screws in, one for each side, and carefully placed the work on the wall. When it was up, he hopped off the couch, drill still in hand, and joined the group for a full look. The four stood in a line in the late-morning sun and sighed. Donna felt a strange warmth, surrounded by the three most impactful people in her life, for better or for worse.

Joshua seemed to like the work, too. After seeing it up in its completed vision, he patted Cole's shoulder once and said, "Thanks, man."

Donna looked over at Cole and he looked back at her. They had won, arrived at some closure at last, and shared a private smile in their triumph. Donna couldn't believe anything that had happened. It was like an eon had passed in the time since the time she'd met Cole at the bar. Beneath all the madness that went down, she still thought of him as nothing but great. And funny, and weird. In that moment, Donna realized her adoration for Cole had become even stronger in its evolution. The vicissitudes were just part of it, and the two were just as connected as they had been on their first night.

Cole handed Joshua the drill back to put in the box. What happened next was like a slow, confusing night terror.

The drill whirred on high speed. In one fierce movement, Joshua pinned Cole against the couch, right up against the painting, and pushed the spinning drill straight into his skull.

CHAPTER TWENTY-NINE: THE MIDWEST

Cole tried to call to Donna to save him, but he was gone in an instant. Joshua had made a perfect hole in the center of Cole's forehead but kept going, drilling all the way through, as though he wanted to hang Cole right up on the wall with the picture. The noise kept droning loud alongside the women's shrieks and screams while Joshua stayed focused, silent, a man busy decorating his home.

To Donna, it all looked like a flip book. Every image was a severely disjointed flash of events. In one second, the painting was crashing to the floor, and in the next, there was a sickening scream, and then a deafening crunch, and then there was the sound of Cole's skull breaking apart. It was like a stone sculpture being dropped to the floor. Parts of Cole were matted into Donna's hair and over her mother's face, and the rest of him splattered like wine all over his beautiful painting.

Donna fell to her knees and started to vomit. She couldn't stop. She wanted to run to her mother and beg for help. She wanted to break the painting into a billion little bits like confetti all around the house. She wanted to burn the house down. She wanted to find Joshua's mother and slay her. Completely obliterate her. Leave her for dead. But most of all, she wanted to murder Joshua. She wanted to murder him in the most painful way anyone could murder a person. She didn't know what could be more painful than driving a drill into someone's skull, but she wanted to find it. At some point, she heard her mother wrestling with Joshua over the gun. In the end, the bullets were thrown all about — a frenzy of bullets of blood and screws and body parts.

And the painting.

The goddamn, motherfucking cream-colored painting that was just splattered in red.

* * *

Two women on their way to a late-morning hike called the police, citing ungodly screams and what appeared to be a physical altercation in the front window.

When the cops arrived, Donna was lying at Joshua's feet sobbing and scratching his calves over and over with her fingernails. It was all she could muster in her shock, a few pathetic scrapes and scratches, but she was grateful to make him bleed at all. He stood completely still — his expression blank and unremorseful — with his signature front-pocket shirt soaked in blood.

As the police report put it, Joshua was the clear perpetrator and got quickly escorted to the police station. Donna and Addie weren't allowed to shower for what felt like the eternity of hell, their bodies prodded and picked at by strangers while Cole's fluids and remains crusted against their skin. Donna demanded his remains be treated like royalty — she didn't know where they were going, but he deserved the burial of a king. When she finally showered in the pathetic hospital bathroom, she felt ill watching the last parts of him leave her and swirl down the drain.

After days of grueling questions, Donna told her mother, "I want to go home with you to Chicago, and I don't want to leave until I die one day."

"We will get past this," Addie said. She had to say that, but she was facing psychological troubles of her own. PTSD settled into her soul quickly and furiously. She did end up going to therapy — as she explained to Donna, all she could think about when she closed her eyes was that beer she had shared with Cole and how she felt like he was such an impressionable young man. She admitted that even a dark part of her even felt a kind of romance for him, or more so a longing for a partner in her life that she never had. She didn't want to beat herself up over that. Sure, it was strange, but she was Donna's mother, after all. They were entwined. They had so much in common.

Drunkenness was now triggering to Donna, so she stayed sober as much as possible. But the two did smoke together, and often. Days and months of dreariness passed. Eventually, Addie went back to work. Her company was forgiving about her trauma, to an extent, but they couldn't wrap their minds around her involvement in the whole ordeal. It was hard for people to put together the relationships of it all — her daughter's Craigslist roommate, her daughter's boyfriend. It all sounded eerily impersonal, even though the experience was now rooted in Addie's very blood.

The two women moved into an apartment together. The takeaway from Joshua and Rudy's house and the whole ordeal was that neither woman had been happy to begin with. After it all, it felt as though they had taken precious occurrences for granted, and they blamed themselves. Donna blamed herself for thinking Cole was bland. Her mother blamed herself for complaining so much about her mundane, not-so-bad life. Their self-pity piled up into insurmountable grief.

Donna tried a few different kinds of therapy. She was angry in the therapy that made her relive witnessing Cole's murder. Then, she was angrier at the therapy that didn't have her recall the events at all.

During her recovery, she felt invisible and exposed at the same time. She didn't know what she wanted. Part of her wanted everyone to leave her alone and forget her. Another part needed people to give her attention, to soothe her, to coddle her. The remaining sliver of her just wanted to be dead.

They outsourced a company to fix up the house and sell it. Because this caused bitterness among their relatives, they agreed to split the sale with their primary extended family. It all felt like bullshit, bullshit they didn't want to be dealing with in the wake of their grief. They were preoccupied, to say the least. Thankfully, the house sold quickly. It was in a nice location, and buyers were drawn to its secluded nature. But because of the damage Joshua had done to the house and the crime that had taken place there, it was listed as a "fixer-upper." Grandmother Rudy probably rolled in her grave. After all the work she did — the pristine condition she left it in. But for many buyers, Topanga was already desirable because of its turbulent history. The area had been home to the Manson family for a while, which drew true crime fanatics to its murderous lore. Now, the turquoise bungalow was a part of that seedy tapestry. It became a destination. A horror story. People were so fucked up.

Donna dreamt about the painting. In the dream, she walked into the horse stable, but it was the pretty, abstract version of the horse stable that Cole had created. The dream always started out peacefully. She would go in and pet the horse and see the envelope on the ground. Then, she would lift and open the envelope, and everything would go awry. She would cry uncontrollably and be splattered with blood. The horse would scream and kick its legs. The horse in the dream started off friendly and became terrifying.

She also thought about Cole, alone in his studio, painting the artwork. At the end of his life, Donna wasn't sure what Cole had painted the picture for. She wondered if it was because he wanted to prove his friendship to her. Or if he felt obligated. If she bullied and manipulated him into doing it. Maybe he just wanted to be a part of the excitement. But hopefully, and Donna held this close to her heart, hopefully he had some kind of feeling of romantic love for her that he carried into his death.

After his death, Donna felt like he had been The One. She mourned the loss of him as if he were her husband. And she couldn't blame herself for that. Everything was a constant question of "could-have-beens." She wasn't even out of bed in the mornings before he crossed her mind. Everything he had ever said suddenly seemed to be so important. She tried to recall every second but couldn't, because in the memories she was stressed about Joshua or she was drunk or she was just . . . elsewhere. Thinking about the salon. Griping. Watching stupid television. She wanted to go back in time and study his face and every movement as closely as she could. She wanted to go back and ask him out to paint. He could have taught her, and she could have kept it going.

They gave everything of Rudy's away to charity and threw Joshua's belongings in the trash. Donna considered sending the "Mom" box to his actual mother but decided she didn't deserve it. She didn't deserve anything except to rot in hell. She was an awful person who caused another person to be awful, too. At least, that was the narrative that gave Donna peace.

Ricky and Melanie hadn't turned into sociopathic murderers, so it was possible Joshua was born with his mania. But Donna had a hard time accepting that. Surely, some people in the world were just rotten — but to what extent does that eradicate responsibility for one's misdoings? She didn't want to feel sorry for Joshua. She wanted to hate his guts. But that was another ailment of Donna's grief — her compassion.

She tried and tried her hardest to wish Joshua were dead. At the scene of the crime, she wanted to strangle him or put a spell on him that would make him disappear. Now, she thought about him and felt numb. And she was so furious that she remembered Joshua more vividly than she could remember Cole. She remembered Joshua's face exactly — his movements, his laugh, his scanning eyes. He always looked like he was up to something, even when he was on his best behavior.

The murder of Cole was perceived as a crime of passion.

Donna perceived it as a premeditated crime. So did Addie. But Addie began to face alcohol troubles of her own, further muddying the boundaries of the two's complicated relationship. Everything made her disassociate. It was just too much.

One refreshing thing that happened was that Lydia came to visit. Donna was comforted to see her. Everyone at the salon was worried. Apparently, the place was different once Donna stopped coming in, answering calls, lighting up the room.

"I never lit up the room," Donna said. "Ever."

"Oh yes you did," said Lydia. "You never take the time to see how great you are." Donna was confused — all this time, she had seen herself as a big loser. She felt like she was in a constant cycle of self-sabotage. "You're the first person to get the promised benefits of that job. Most people leave after a month or so, treating the place like a joke. You are special because you care." Donna had cared about that job, and it was true that she had given it her all. Lydia taking notice of her efforts reminded her what a true friend was — it wasn't someone who indulged in toxicity. It was someone who challenged and supported her. Someday, she planned to pay the generosity back.

Before she left, Lydia gave Donna a fresh cut and color. Rather than going with any neon highlights, she went for a nice, clean-looking blonde. It hung effortlessly above Donna's collar bones and made her look more put together than she had in months. As she looked at herself in the mirror, she smiled gently. Something about her new 'do made her feel less hopeless.

Despite the burst of positivity Lydia brought, she also ragged on Chicago the whole time. "I left her for a reason," she said. "And you should, too." She begged Donna not to stay too long, saying that she would freeze there, into a cold dust. Donna couldn't make any promises. For all she knew, she would be there forever and ever, and even buried there, amen.

CHAPTER THIRTY: MAPS

One Saturday morning, about a year after the murder, Donna and Addie sat on the sofa eating bagels and lox and watching television. They didn't talk much — to each other or to anyone else. They lived in almost total seclusion but were grateful for each other's company as roommates. The house phone rang which was strange. No one used the house phone anymore except telemarketers.

It was Donna's second cousin, on her father's side. She wanted Donna and Addie to know that Aunt Sheeba had died. She had been sick during the last year, and the disease caught up rapidly.

Donna felt a sharp pain in her stomach. Aunt Sheeba had been so helpful to her. Without her, she would have never known that Joshua had a relationship with Grandma Rudy. She would have never known Joshua used aliases. And she was sad to hear she passed, because she had never even properly thanked her. But in contrast to how she felt when Rudy died, she felt grateful that she had made an effort with Sheeba. She did go visit her in Thousand Oaks. She did cultivate a kind of unique kinship. This was the first death Donna experienced that wasn't riddled with too many regrets.

"You should go to the memorial," her mother told her.

Donna knew the memorial would be in Thousand Oaks, and the idea of boarding a plane and going back west — to be around death and grieving people — crippled her. "I can't go back there," was her knee-jerk reaction. "It's too much."

"Donna," Addie reasoned. "I know it will be difficult, but think of how much it would mean to her if you went to her service."

Donna was surprised. She didn't think her mother was aware of the intricacies between Donna and Sheeba's relationship, but she guessed she had spoken of her fondly.

"Mom," said Donna. "I'm not ready to be around death."

"No one is, hon," Addie said. "I know. Especially not me and especially not you, but it's the right thing to do. How about I go with you?"

Donna agreed, even though she felt worried about it. She thought about Sheeba often and hadn't been able to say goodbye properly. After the murder, Sheeba and Donna emailed a bit about everything that happened. But truthfully, Donna couldn't bring herself to talk too much about it and, in some ways, Sheeba felt responsible. She even confessed she wished she'd forked up some cash for Donna to get a lawyer. But in the end, cash hadn't been the problem — it was Donna's own drive for revenge that screwed her.

The day to travel to the funeral arrived, and neither woman knew what to wear. Donna was sick about flying to California again. She now saw it as the darkest, most unholy place on the planet. She didn't even bring her pink Polaroid camera with her. All she had left of California was the photo Cole had taken of her in front of the house. And more than once, she had the urge to burn that photo and forget she could ever smile in such a terrible place. But she didn't — she tugged it away in her trauma place, her high school yearbook, folded alongside the AIM conversation that signified her father's death.

* * *

Once they arrived at the house, their relatives moved out of their clusters of conversation. There was a breakfast at Aunt Sheeba's Thousand Oaks ranch-style house before the group was to move to a nearby Presbyterian church for the service.

Where there were pockets of community, a line now formed, a wall. The wall faced Donna. She looked at each of their faces. They looked bewildered, concerned, curious. Donna looked down at her clothes. She wondered if she was not dressed appropriately for a memorial. But her stockings and black, tea-length sack seemed to fit the bill. She wondered what her face looked like but decided her tinted lip balm was appropriate. She wasn't wearing heels. She knew they weren't judging her for her appearance so much as the trail of chaos and unruliness that followed behind her. Surely she was a problem if she attracted squatters and murderers. Because she and Addie were estranged from that side of the family, the relatives lacked compassion. The one exception, of course, was Sheeba.

In the wake of her humiliation, she rushed off to the bathroom. In the cold powder room, she stared into the mirror and cursed herself. When had she become so hideous, so vacant, so stupid? Her skin looked cracked from lack of moisturizer. Her nails were grubby and her legs were hairy. She was a poster child for depression and grief. She spat on the mirror and wished the spit could make her reflection disappear.

When she finally left the bathroom, her mother looked impatient.

"Donna, can you come here, please?" Addie asked. Donna set the bouquet she held on the foyer table. What seemed like a nice gesture now seemed stupid. The sunflowers didn't look very fresh, after all.

She crept after her mother, full of dread, feeling heavier with each step. When they got outside, the air was humid. Small strands from Donna's low ponytail blew into her face. Addie dug a cigarette from her clutch and took an eternity to find a light. Finally, she ripped a tiny, lavender lighter from the mess. Donna held up her hands to cover the wind. Addie inhaled and held in the smoke for several seconds before blowing it out.

"What's going on?" Donna asked.

"Do you want one?" Addie asked.

Donna felt stressed. "Sure." In the damp air, tiny drops of cool rain began to fall. Donna remembered how little it rained in LA. Of course it would rain as soon as she arrived. Donna pressed on. "Mom?"

"Donna, everyone is talking."

"I'm sure," Donna said. "I'm sure I messed up everything. I'm sure the legacy of the house, or whatever, wasn't what everyone had hoped." She was firm. "I did the best I could. I did."

Addie was taken aback. "That's not what I mean."

"Then what?" Donna asked. "What? Everyone is on edge today? Anxious? Well yeah, it's a memorial service."

"Honey," her mom started, "Is there something you're not telling me about your relationship with Aunt Sheeba?"

Donna melted a little. "I guess," she said.

"I know you were close," Addie continued, "but how close?"

Donna felt embarrassed. She didn't know what to say. She didn't want to talk about Joshua on this day — she couldn't get sucked down by memories while she was trying to hold it together for the service. Her first thought was that someone had uncovered the information about Joshua in Sheeba's house. Sheeba had collected a wide range of evidence — surely she had put it away somewhere when she was sick. Donna's fear was that it was being passed around at the memorial gathering.

"Listen." Addie interrupted her thoughts and looked into the dark windows of the house. A row of family members watched their conversation in suspense. "Everyone is talking about you," she went on. "Everyone is talking about you because Aunt Sheeba left you her house."

Donna started to laugh. She started to laugh so hard she cried, almost, the smoke puffing out of her lungs with every release of laughter. "You've got to be fucking kidding," she said.

"Is that funny to you?" Addie asked. "Because it sure wasn't funny the first go-around."

"It is funny," Donna said. "It is. Wow."

Aunt Sheeba's house. In many ways, it was the opposite of Rudy's. It was a tan ranch type, completely unadorned, but spacious. It sat on an airy lot of land with lots of sun and no trees. Rather than a cottage nestled in a wood, it was masculine — practical, unstylized. She couldn't imagine living there. It was more in line with Addie's taste.

"Are you going to accept it?" Addie wanted to know.

"Mom," Donna said, "I have no fucking clue." She paused for a while. The information came at an inopportune time. Soon, they'd grab their purses and head to the church in a black car, with family members who resented her doubly. "If I don't take it, what then?"

"Then I guess you'll decide, I don't know, I guess we'll decide who you want to give it to. With guidance."

"Okay," Donna said.

"What?" her mom asked.

"I want to give it to you."

Addie laughed, too. Hard.

"I'm serious."

"And what?"

"What do you mean 'and what'?" Donna pushed. "You'll live in it."

"What am I going to do living in it?" Addie asked.

"You'll keep it nice," Donna said.

"And what about you? What good is it going to be with you in Chicago when I'm all the way out here?"

"I'll be your roommate," Donna said. "I'll be your roommate for a little while."

Addie thought for a while.

"What if I don't want to keep being your roommate?"

Donna shook her head, took one last inhale of her cigarette and stomped it out. "Let's go in."

They went in, past the row of speculating family, and to the back wall, where the door to Aunt Sheeba's room stood wide open. Inside the room, it was quaint. The scent was peaceful. It was like fresh rolls of tissue paper, the inside of metal perfume boxes, the old wood of a vanity. In the mirror, there were splotches of hair spray and dainty little fingerprints. In the made bed, the comforter wrinkled, but just a little. As if Aunt Sheeba sat down recently and tied her shoes, or organized her purse. On the pillow, a faint head mark. Where she had lain, so recently.

"What if the open casket was in here?" Donna joked.

"I'd stay far away," Addie said. She breathed the room in. "I'll think about it."

As they were leaving the room, Donna saw a large, galvanized lockbox that had her name on it. She didn't know where the key was — it was a new mystery to solve. But without opening the contents, she knew what it was. It was all their detective work, hidden securely for Donna's eyes only. She smiled and whispered a "thank you" to Aunt Sheeba. She was sorry she was gone but grateful to have known her. Like Cole with his parents. For the first time, death made sense.

Donna's cell rang, startling her. She hesitated before answering, as the number was unknown. Shaking, she finally did, right before it reached her voicemail. It was an automated call. The robot on the other line said it was a prepaid call from the county prison. It prompted her to decide to speak to an inmate in the jail. The inmate's name was Donovan Sandoval.

To speak to him, she would press one. To ignore the call, she would press two.

She closed her eyes and pictured herself on one of those old maps of the United States of America in all its geographical glory. On the map, there were childlike illustrations of the different regions. The mountains, the rolling plains, the prairies. At cities, there were little pictures of skyscrapers and boardwalks. Around where she was in California, the Hollywood sign and canyons and tiny pictures of iced coffees. Sand, waves and bike trails. She thought of the illustrations of her own California. Dark paths and loneliness. Drunkenness. Dead trees and high cliffs. She thought about her pink Polaroid and Cole and how it felt to be wanted. On her mind map, she saw an illustration of a woman who felt like a girl lying in bed all alone.

She pushed two.

THE END

ACKNOWLEDGMENTS

Thank you so much to everyone who read this book in all its drafts and encouraged me along the way. I especially want to thank the mentors and friends I met at DePaul University, including Ted Anton, Rebecca Johns-Trissler and Kathleen Rooney for all their guidance and time on this book and so many more of my projects.

I also want to thank friends, including Naomi Huffman, Juli Hurtado, Luci Lyle, Rachel Robbins, Jewells Santos, Alexa Stark and all the others who were integral to the book's editorial vision and process.

Thank you to my mom, dad, siblings, grandparents, aunts, uncles, cousins, friends and teachers that inspired and encouraged me to keep at the writing thing. Thank you to Stephanie Bong and Cody Koehler for teaching me about snakes. And thank you to my friend Sam Straley for being a great collaborator on my vision.

Thank you to the fabulous editor, Steph Carey, and publisher Jasper Joffe for taking the book on and really "getting" it. Thank you to my agent, Alicia Brooks, at the Jean V. Nagger Literary Agency. And big thanks to the writer William Brennan, who wrote the essay in *New York Mag* that sent me into a research spiral about squatters' rights.

And lastly, a huge thank you to my husband, Andy, and my son, Augie, for always giving me time and space to create.

Thank you for reading this book.

If you enjoyed it please leave feedback on Amazon or Goodreads, and if there is anything we missed or you have a question about, then please get in touch. We appreciate you choosing our book.

Founded in 2014 in Shoreditch, London, we at Joffe Books pride ourselves on our history of innovative publishing. We were thrilled to be shortlisted for Independent Publisher of the Year at the British Book Awards.

www.joffebooks.com

We're very grateful to eagle-eyed readers who take the time to contact us. Please send any errors you find to corrections@joffebooks.com. We'll get them fixed ASAP.

Made in the USA
Coppell, TX
25 August 2022

82057220R00129